Tales Spun
by the Setting Sun

by

Students of
La Quinta High School

La Quinta High School
Westminster, California

Tales Spun by the Setting Sun

Edited and compiled by: Amanda LaPera
Copy Editors: Jenny Nguyen, Kellan Nguyen, Kevin Nguyen
Section Editors: Ruby Chau, Orbal Farhad, Jeslyn Le, Jenny Nguyen, Kellan Nguyen, Kevin Nguyen, Audrey Pham, Jessica Truong, Hailey Zuniga
Cover Designed by: Jessica Truong
Interior Editor: Audrey Pham

Published by La Quinta High School Creative Writing Program

Dedicated to the writers of the future

TABLE OF CONTENTS

INK 1

POEM BY ORBAL FARHAD

CONFESSIONS FROM A SINNER TO A SAINT 2

POEM BY KELLAN NGUYEN

THE GLASS 5

POEM BY KEVIN LE

WHAT WE'VE DONE 6

POEM BY JENNY NGUYEN

PETRA 7

STORY BY ORBAL FARHAD

PEOPLE WATCHING 14

POEM BY RUBY CHAU

THE CRIMSON CONVULSION 16

POEM BY ETHAN HO

A LIFELINE'S LUSTER 18

STORY BY KEVIN NGUYEN

NATURAL DEATH IS NOT BLOODLESS 23

POEM BY ORBAL FARHAD

DISPARITY 24

POEM BY IMAN USMAN

ENEMY GROUNDS 25

STORY BY VIVIAN VU

TORRENTIAL EVENTS 30

POEM BY ETHAN HO

WHERE I'M FROM 31

POEM BY HAILEY ZUNIGA

DEAR AMMIE 32

STORY BY AUDREY PHAM

LIVE LIKE LEGENDS 34

POEM BY TERESA LE

FRAGMENTS 35

POEM BY TERESA LE

IN PLAIN SIGHT 36

STORY BY AUDREY PHAM

FORGETFULNESS 40

POEM BY HAILEY ZUNIGA

THE BRIDE AND THE BRIMSTONE 41

POEM BY KEVIN NGUYEN

FOR I HAVE SINNED 42

STORY BY JESSICA TRUONG

FNET = MA 46

POEM BY TRACY VO

THE GEODE 48

POEM BY KEVIN LE

OH, HOW THE MIGHTY FALL 49

STORY BY KELLAN NGUYEN

THE LAKE OF YOU 65

POEM BY RUBY CHAU

EIGHT AM RUMINATIONS OF A SINNER 66

POEM BY ELEM VU

DESIDERIUM 68

STORY BY JESSICA TRUONG

GODHOOD IN AMERICA 78

POEM BY ELEM VU

A MOTHER'S LOVE 82

POEM BY KELLAN NGUYEN

GLIMPSE OF A KALEIDOSCOPE 84

STORY BY JESLYN LE

WHAT I POUR MY HEART INTO 95

POEM BY JENNY NGUYEN

PARTING 96

POEM BY JESLYN LE

SEE YOU NEXT TIME! 98

POEM BY JESLYN LE

STARCROSSED 99

POEM BY KEVIN NGUYEN

AUTHOR BIOS 101

INK

by Orbal Farhad

What is tongue from tooth?
Or duck from goose?

What is life from death?
A gasp from a breath?

A dying embrace does not differ
From the first sun of spring.
The dance of life and death concur—
And so, too, the spread of wings.

A song that bambino sings,
The only song they knew.
The same song the widow speaks,
Regressed to that same tune.

CONFESSIONS FROM A SINNER TO A SAINT

by Kellan Nguyen

Love, to you, must feel like summer.

Watermelon slices savored to the rind,

Seeds sprinkling the ground like stars.

Roasted lotus seeds crunched between baby teeth and chubby hands,

The warm tingle of being kissed by a mother,

And the rush of air from being carried on the shoulder of a father—

Watching the sky above in an awe that only a child could have.

Devoid of the chill of loneliness, empty of yearning for constancy,

Free from the shackles of expectations.

There were days when I didn't remember if I ever knew what love was.

Or if I did, it must have been one-sided, unrequited and unfulfilled,

And I was tired of pulling my hair out just to try to get someone to

understand me.

To be seen is to be loved, but I sit in a room with a locked door and no

windows.

The walls are thin, so I claw my way through the wood to find light

Only to be left with jagged splinters and bloody hands.

For the longest time,

Love, or maybe the lack thereof,

Felt like the heat of a fresh kill: splashes of crimson on my face,

The sweet tang of revenge that chokes me and leaves only a bitterness
That cannot be washed away.

Oh, how awful it is to love something
That can be so easily taken away.

Now—love, to me, feels like you.
Tart mulberries broken open over my tongue, sweetened by your
presence,
The cool touch of my fingertips pressed into the silkiness of your hair.
When I think of love, I think of your kindness and your righteous fury,
Your wit and your mistakes, and sometimes,
I think I'd burn the world for you.
I would doom everyone else to a wretched fate
Just to write a requiem for your radiance.
I've already been damned for so long,
So what's a few lifetimes more?

But you would never ask me to.
I am a sinner and I love you destructively in a way
Only a monster can.
But for you, I want to try.
And yes, maybe this will end, and maybe
The world will crash and burn
Tomorrow, or the day after, or even today.

But right now, you are in my arms,
Head tucked against my chest, and I can feel

The steady rise and fall of your breath like ocean waves.
Being alive on this earth is a terrible, tragic thing,
But if it means being gifted with your presence,
Then I am glad to have been blessed.

Right now, I am holding your hand under the covers
And I can only remember the unfulfilled ache
For a mother's touch and a father's love,
So, I hold you closer.
Right now, I love you
And you love me in return.
That is enough.

THE GLASS
by Kevin Le

I drank poison so easily
like I have many times before,
gulping down cups of guilt and gratification.
My heart turned black
but I kept coming back
to pain.

You did nothing but smile with that awful loving face,
letting me drink you again,
again,
again,
again,
that fiery drink again.

I drank poison so easily.
I kept coming back
to you.

What We've Done

by Jenny Nguyen

Those Notes

Idle words at bay

Ready to leave the mouth and

Out to inflict pain

Those Types

A person may stay

Or turn their back on the world

To leave and betray

Those Looks

Eyes full of pity

Fall down on feeble faces

Yet hands remain still

PETRA

by Orbal Farhad

I WAS IN A CAB on the way to my hotel, leaning my head out of the window and gazing at the stars. Tonight, it seemed as if they were dancing with the wind and clouds.

"It never gets this cold in the summer," said the young cab driver. He glanced at me through the side view mirror. "Looks like it'll rain, too."

I jerked my head up. "You speak English?"

"Yes, ma'am. Most of us do." The cab driver rolled up the window. "Is this your first time in Jordan?"

"Is it that obvious?"

"Your looks say you're Arab, but I know an American when I see one," he said. His accent reminded me of my father's mother. It was the way he said American. *Amma-Rican.*

"Yeah, this is my first time," I said. "My parents were raised here, and I've always wanted to visit."

It wasn't fate that I was here. I lived in America, in the southern Californian suburbs. My dad fought for the life we have now, but it began to feel like windchimes and mailmen were all I'd ever known. I was desperate to feel a sense of belonging.

BRRRING. BRRRING. My phone sang a sick, ear-piercing tune. BRRRING. BRRRING. I rummaged through my purse to find it and accepted the call. BRRRI—

"Fai?" I said. "You changed my ringtone, didn't you?"

My half-sister was on the other line. "Petra! Why did it take me so long to get you? Are you safe? Do you have your luggage? Do you feel sick? Was it motion sickness? God, I knew you'd have motion sickness. I told you to take my meds. They're perfectly legal."

"One, no, they're not. And two, I'm completely fine. I'm on my way to the hotel. I was just watching the clouds and having a chat with the driver," I replied, smiling at him. He did not return the gesture.

"Yeah, *Khalto* told me. I can't believe it, they said it was beautiful all week. Then suddenly, a rush of clouds came in from the west."

"Hopefully, it's a fluke. I'm gonna see the architecture in *Wadi Musa* all day tomorrow."

"Take pictures for us, okay, Bug? Everyone says hi."

"Tell them I said hi back. Love you." I shut my phone off and turned back to the stars. The driver and I didn't speak for the rest of the ride.

He dropped me off at my shabby little hotel just a few miles outside of Petra, and I thanked him. Tomorrow was sure to be an adventure. Hopefully a sunny one, at that.

* * *

I truly never thought I'd visit my namesake in the flesh. The city I had seen only in photographs from a sentimental grandmother stared at me, and I stared right back. Petra, or *Al-Batra,* as my father would call her.

Thankfully it wasn't raining, but the weather was still gloomy and unlike the Jordan I grew up hearing about. Was my company so unwanted in the city?

I would've thought so if not for the desert dust. It blew into my eyes, against my skin, and found its way beneath my fingertips. It felt like Petra, the city, wanted me to know she would be with me, regardless of whether I chose to stay or leave.

8

Even then, I couldn't help but feel intimidated by her presence. I was exposed before a city I knew had seen God but been subjected to exasperated tourists and self-proclaimed prophets—all usurpers in their own ways. One came towards me as I appreciated the architecture.

"Ma'am?" the man asked. "Ma'am, is that you?" I noticed his unique Jordanian drawl. He walked closer and became less of a man and more of a boy.

"I suppose it depends on who you're looking for."

"Last night. The American." *Amma-Rican.* "You said your name was …"

"Petra."

The cab driver extended a hand, but I shook my head apologetically, holding out my splayed hands. They were brown with dust.

"Yes, yes, Petra. That's why I figured I'd find you here."

"You came here to find me?"

"No, I wouldn't say that. I don't know why I came here, actually. Something compelled me to. Then I saw a woman from afar, shielding her face from the sand, and I couldn't shake the feeling it might have been you."

We exchanged a smile. He began walking with me as I explored *Wadi Musa,* the "Lost City." The more popular architecture was built over older work, but there was still plenty to see.

"Is this little town all you came for, Ma'am?"

"I suppose so, yes," I replied. "I have some aunts and uncles that I'll see on my final day here, but I have no plans besides seeing the land my father loved so dearly that he named his daughter after it. I was hoping it might make me feel better about being so out of place in California."

"It's sad to hear you're not planning on seeing more of Jordan," he said.

"How come?"

"I've been a driver for a long time. For Americans, for Brits, for Palestinians. Ironically, my passengers are rarely Jordanians themselves, but…I've never felt so compelled to tell someone about my favorite spot."

9

He stopped speaking for a moment, putting his hand on my shoulder. "Perhaps it's because you're a Jordanian-American and this is your first time here or because the clouds came the moment I picked you up. Whatever it may be, I feel I need to tell you this."

"Tell me," I said, but I backed away. I was startled by his boldness—I'd never heard of locals being so audacious with tourists.

He gave me a reassuring smile. "Let me take you to *al-Bahir al-Mayyit.*"

"The Dead Sea?"

* * *

I'd been defying every law of the land, every piece of advice I'd received from my family, but this man's sincerity had bewitched me. The charm of this young cab driver, whose name I had yet to learn, was too enthralling to ignore.

We were on our way to The Dead Sea, a three-hour drive that might have been grueling if not for the striking sight of the desert or the fervor of the young man as he told me stories of him and his friends swimming in the sea on the hottest of summer days.

"Here we are," he said, stepping out of the car. "Do you know why we call it The Dead Sea?"

I shook my head.

"Well," he began, "the saltiness of the sea, it's too much to bear for any plant or animal that finds themselves yearning for a body of water to reside in. They could step into the sea for a home, only to die moments later."

"I didn't know that. Is it ... is it safe for humans?" I asked.

"Yes, of course. In biblical times, people would visit the sea in hopes of curing illness. Although my mother had another theory. She said Jordanians would enter and feel enlightened, but tourists that entered the sea would leave cursed. That, or they wouldn't leave at all."

10

"Well … am I a Jordanian or a tourist?"

He didn't answer my question. Instead, he pointed to the sea. "I think you should get in. It can heal your wounds."

"How do you know I have wounds?"

"We all have wounds," he replied cryptically.

I was unsettled, but I couldn't deny my curiosity. Stepping out of my sandals, I made my way to the water. It was the lightest of blues and sparkled in the sun's embrace, the shore and seabed adorned with jagged rocks of salt. I dipped a toe in, and as if it was fate, the clouds above me deepened into a stormy gray and began to rain on me.

I turned back to the driver, but he only gestured for me to continue. So I did. I walked further into the water. And further. And further.

Before I knew it, my entire body was submerged into the water, all but my head. I took a breath, though it felt like I hadn't breathed in ages. I was underwater, but it was more like I was under a boulder, pressing me into the seabed. I brought my head up, or rather, I *tried* to bring my head up. I tried to push my legs out of the water. I tried to.

Was this how I wanted to reunite with my homeland?

As I struggled in the waves, I thought about my father. My mother. Fai. And the others too. What would become of them if I disappeared?

My scattered thoughts came back to the day we stepped foot on American soil.

Dad wanted a better future for all of us. He had worked so hard, but had we really made it that far? Without Mom, there was still a piece missing, a piece I had yet to find in my trip across the Earth.

And then a voice resonated from the depths. It was booming yet feminine. Although I could not catch the words, her voice washed a sense of relief over me. It was like I was in my mother's arms once more.

Finally, I came up coughing and gasping for breath. I noticed immediately that the clouds had cleared and that the driver and the voice were nowhere to be seen.

"Hello?" I yelled as I brought myself to the shore. "Is anybody here?" He was not in his cab which sat vacant. I could not find a man or mouse for the mile that I'm sure I walked while drenched in saltwater.

* * *

I was back in Petra. I commandeered the man's cab and rushed to *Wadi Musa,* the only other place my heart told me where I might expect to find him. Adrenaline pumped through my body with every step I took towards the Lost City.

But again, there was no one. No cars on the road. No falafel vendors, no usurpers, no cab-drivers. I stepped outside, surrounded by the surreal silence of the desert air.

"Petra!" A familiar booming voice erupted from behind me. "You've finally shown yourself before your mother. Why did it take you so long to find me?" I nearly spun myself to death trying to spot the location of the voice.

"Stop spinning your head. I am the Earth. I am the dust. I am the desert and the sea. I am Petra, and I am the Mother of Jordan."

"You're the mother of Jordan?" I stopped searching and sank to my knees. "But I don't have a mother. Not anymore." I couldn't shake off the familiarity of the voice.

"I know, just as I know of all. I felt your presence as soon as you landed in the airport, so I told another child of mine to meet you and bring you to the sea so that you could see me," said the voice.

"The taxi driver is your son? Does that make him my brother?"

12

"All motherless Jordanian children are my children. You came to Jordan in hopes of finding what you have missed. I wouldn't have found you if you were not lost."

"I'm sorry," I said. My voice began to crack, like my bold front as a woman. "I don't know what to do now. How am I supposed to go back to America now that I know that my home is here, that *you're* here?"

The voice was quiet as if she were deep in thought. There was no perfect answer to my question. She began in a soft tone, "Petra, my dear. My intention was never to confuse you, it was to enlighten you. Do you know why your father named you Petra?"

Though I felt I had the answer, I shook my head.

"Your father named you after me because he had the same set of ideals as I do. I know you were raised in America without a mother, and that hurt you greatly, but what a mother is, and what a home is, there was never any confusion to me. A girl's mother is her heart, and a home is not a place *you* live. It is where your heart resides."

"What does that mean?" I asked her.

"It means that I am your mother and your home, so you will no longer have to feel like you have neither in America. Let my existence be your freedom."

PEOPLE WATCHING

by Ruby Chau

I see the tension

In the way you look at her.

Your eyes cannot pull away

From the lips that are moving,

From the smile that is growing.

Everyone in this room can see it.

I see the tension

In the way she looks at you.

Her eyes light up with joy,

She can't help but lean closer to you.

Everyone here can see it.

It must feel nice to be in love.

To have your heart skip a beat,

To have your cheeks warm up,

To have someone to hold on to,

To have someone you are afraid to lose,

To have someone break your heart,

And fix it, over and over.

But here I am watching,
Wondering if this is just
An ephemeral moment.

People come and go.
How do you know
If this will even last?

THE CRIMSON CONVULSION
by Ethan Ho

The trees bowed,
The animals grazed,
And the grass danced with pride.

That was, until a great foreign presence corrupted the land.
Each blade of grass and leaf upon the canopy,
desecrated in thick scarlet.

Adhesive, and hard to remove.
The day flesh fell from the sky, everything changed.

A peaceful valley began to writhe and grow ravenous,
All fauna warping into carnivorous monsters.

With each step, a hungry set of jaws leapt from the ground,
The warbles of life, the rustle of lush leaves,
the pitter patter of small mammals.

Silenced,

Degraded into savage, guttural cries,

Emitted by the infected land,

And a disturbing, wet, meshing sound,

A constant white noise.

As if the land itself was in pain,

Devoid of any definition of nature.

A biosphere converted from herbivory to carnism.

A LIFELINE'S LUSTER

by Kevin Nguyen

I WAS DEAD. Or at least, I was supposed to be. The car came out of nowhere, didn't it? It couldn't have been my fault, right? So, please, deities of the afterlife, have mercy. But where was I anyway?

A blank limbo. As I tentatively wriggled my fingertips, pins and needles sprung up throughout my body. I couldn't see either. One moment, I was hurling through the air with the thundering sound of a car horn fading away, and then I was slammed onto some kind of surface.

My eyes adjusted. I blinked several times, pinching and pulling my face to confirm that I was alive. In front of me was a door painted white on traditional wood.

"Hello?" I croaked from my sprawled position on the floor.

But there was no answer.

I embraced my legs gingerly and wobbled off the ground. My body faltered and my vision blurred. Was I dead? Was this Heaven? Or Hell? Or some Lovecraftian hex?

Something creaked beneath my feet, and I flinched. The sound continued, louder than before. Taking another cautious step forward, I noticed that it played with each step.

I braced myself to charge through the daunting hallway. What was the worst that could happen? Dying again?

My feet leapt into action, and I squinted at the door that lurched forward with my approach. I continued the dash into the blinding curtain of light and collapsed face-first onto something soft.

It would be a lie to say I didn't feel like I had died all over again. A shriek escaped from my mouth as I crashed back onto the bedroom floor of my apartment. My head flew backward, and I stared at the wide-open closet.

Didn't I die? Why was I back at home? How?

These questions lured me to the window. I pulled away the curtains and took a look outside the bustling city streets.

I screamed again.

In the place of ordinary citizens and passersby, was me. They were all "me." Everybody donned my face, my features, my everything. Although their outfits and actions varied, they were all me.

"This ... this really is Hell, isn't it?" I whimpered, burying half of my pale face behind the curtain. The city was just how I remembered it, but everyone was identical, identical to me.

I raced into the kitchen and grabbed my knife, taking notice of the destroyed tables and chairs that littered the room. I needed a barricade. I needed to survive. Panicking didn't help, but I hyperventilated. The windows. How would I guard them? What if those things could fly? What *were* those things? Where was the—

Knock, knock.

I stared at the door in horror. They were here. It was over for me. Gripping my knife with frozen knuckles, I prepared for yet another death.

My replicated voice echoed from the other side. "Excuse me? Are you the new arrival?"

Arrival? Who was this man pretending to be me?

"St-stay away, I'm armed!"

"I'm afraid what you're doing is pointless. Please, come out."

"And what then? You'll kill me?" I stood up and scoured the room for anything that could help. Anything that could—

Click.

19

The apartment front door was forced open, and the pitiful clutter of furniture stacked against it knocked aside. He walked into the room and stared at me quivering in the corner. He raised his hands in surrender upon noticing the knife. "I'm sure you're scared. And confused. But I promise you, I have the answers that you're—"

"Get out!"

The man smiled. "I can't do that. You see, in order for me to become the next *Pilot,* I have to touch the forehead of the previous Pilot."

Then, the television flickered to life. We were both silent for a moment, watching what "I" was saying on the sudden broadcast.

"Attention, all residents. Pilot #346 has returned. Those who wish for their turn to ascend must head to 142 Westview Apartments, Building C ..."

The other "I" laughed. "You see, that person on the broadcast right now is *you,* living a different life. Or rather, *us.*"

I lowered my weapon. "What are you saying?"

"He is a version of you in which you became a top-star journalist. I, myself, am a version of you in which I became a talented escape artist." He tossed a lock pick across the floor and reached into his back pocket. "Rather confusing, I know. It's best to try not to die on Earth and lose your mortal form, unless you want to return to this place soon. Our counterparts don't have our best interests at heart."

"Who *am* I?"

He chuckled to himself. "It doesn't matter who you are when you're down here. Everyone's been waiting. Waiting for their chance to live a life."

"Please, I don't know what you want with me. I need to go home—"

"Nobody can make a difference here. Not unless you're on Earth amongst others. We live the same lives every day *waiting*. Waiting for the current pilot to die a miserable death and come back here."

My grip on the knife tightened. The man took out a pistol and aimed it at my chest.

"What's going to happen now is that you're going to free me from this cycle. You've had your chance and you squandered it. Why don't you let a more capable version of yourself live Arthur Turner's next life?"

"I *am* Arthur Turner," I screamed back. Not as an act of defiance to the doppelganger in front of me, but for some sense of validation. "None of you are real."

The man laughed for what seemed to be the thousandth time. "Pilots always seem to believe that when they return. They've been gone from here far too long to remember what it was like to be trapped in this cycle of envy. I don't even know how you, of all people, became a Pilot for the vessel. A worthless, mundane copy of me. Don't you feel guilty for how you've taken away a chance at life from so many better versions of you?"

Stomping and shouting erupted by the doorway.

"You're a waste of space. Just let me touch your forehead and you can go back to being useless." He started towards me.

Several identical versions of myself rushed through the front door, eyeing my being that was cowering in the corner. The man swung the pistol back and forth between all of us. "Stay back, he's mine. It's finally my turn." His pace quickened as he reached his hand out to grab me.

Crying out, I lashed at him with the knife.

He retaliated by firing the gun, and my stomach exploded in pain as scarlet poured from the wound. While I keeled over, I could only watch as he, along with the other copies behind him, raced towards my broken figure.

Someone's hand slammed against my forehead and he disappeared in a bright flash of light. Murmurs washed over the room. "It's over ..."

I blinked away the tears that obscured my vision and looked around at the crowd that had just piled into my home. The man with the gun was gone.

I saw myself in different professions. There were veterans, doctors, scientists, bakers, businessmen, people who all were me but in different lives. Some obviously successful, wealthy, famous lives.

21

They were all looking at me, judging me. Was I a failure? How could someone like me ever live as Arthur Turner? These other possible versions of Arthur—they would've done a much better job.

"What happens now?" My hand was still clamped over the gushing wound.

A man in a suit stepped forward. "The escape artist was born as an infant on Earth. Not as Arthur Turner, but as someone new. Soon, we will shift our appearance accordingly. All of us are just possibilities of what that person could become. That newborn infant is thus destined to become an escape artist."

"So I'm stuck here?"

The man ignored my question and turned to the crowd. "There's nothing left for us here. Let's go." He gave me one last pitying look. "Perhaps you should've done something more meaningful with your life."

The door closed. Only sunlight was left in the room to illuminate my bleeding body. The excitement of the Pilot's return disappeared, and life in this world continued.

NATURAL DEATH IS NOT BLOODLESS
by Orbal Farhad

Natural death is not bloodless.

Yes, my grandmother died of old age,
Her frail body could no longer bear the weight of her mind.
After a grueling six months' post-stroke,
The woman died.

There were no bloody fingers,
No gunshots nor bullet wounds.
But still, I will argue
Natural death is not bloodless.

The few of us left
Will never see each other the same.

Perhaps knowing made it worse.
As if a knife was pointed at its victim,
Inching to her face so stealthily,
So slowly
That the rest of us forgot
It would eventually pierce skin.

Natural death is not bloodless.

DISPARITY

by Iman Usman

Disparity, a tale so tragic,
Of riches for the "faultless" and poverty for the "flawed,"
A world divided where fairness is denied,
Leaving behind a trail of pain and misery.

In this world, some live in woe,
Their pockets barren but their faces aglow
With hopelessness and hunger as they endure the road
While the rich bathe in wealth, never knowing the load.

The divide grows broader like a river's span
Weaving its way through a tainted land,
The haves and have-nots stretching an endless game
Where the rich stay rich and the poor remain.

But hope still abides in the hearts of the meek
For a brighter tomorrow where all are equal and free,
Where love and compassion shall reign supreme,
And disparity shall give way to the people's greatest dream.

ENEMY GROUNDS

by Vivian Vu

THERE WAS A CHILL when I woke up, one that seeped under my skin and drilled deep into my bones.

My head throbbed as I slowly sat up on a rough stone bench. My entire cell was made of this same rough stone. A small, barred window cast a square of light on the metal door. Black spots dotted my vision, but even so, I could see a figure of a man pacing across the room, just beyond my bars. He was muttering excitedly to himself, almost in mania.

"I think the ground might wear out if you pace any longer," I told him. "Is this really any way to treat your prisoner?"

He jerked his head up, and from the dim light streaming through the window, I could finally identify him as the same general that had thrown me into this cell. He shot a glare at me. "You are the head of this traitorous rebellion, Archer. I'd keep my mouth shut if I were you."

"Out of all the people to take advice from, I'll have to reconsider your credibility." I leaned back against the wall for support. It was probably unwise to annoy him—I knew this even in my delirious state—but the truth was, I was irritated beyond belief and couldn't bring myself to reason my way out of this.

"Just you wait," he hissed. "When I tell the crown prince about you…"

"Alastor?" I asked. "What about him?"

The man grew impossibly angrier. "It's *Prince* Alastor to you. You faeries are still in his kingdom, living under his laws. To think that not even the mastermind behind the rebel forces can understand this."

"First," I began. "Alastor is *not* my prince. Second, wanting to live isn't a crime. If it is, then it shouldn't be. None of us asked to be a faerie any more than you were 'lucky' to be born a fairy."

The general's jaw clenched so hard that I thought his teeth would crack open. "Shut up. When Prince Alastor grants me permission, you'll suffer the most painful death yet. We'll make sure the rest of your little friends find out about it."

At the idea of my death, glee danced in his flinty eyes. He went on and on about all the fascinating ways I was going to die, speaking faster and faster by the minute. Just when I considered finding a way to make myself deaf to his voice, the metal door creaked open. A familiar voice cut in, thankfully quieting the general.

"Fabien."

He froze. Surprise flashed across his face before it was replaced with a look of greed. "Prince Alastor!"

Alastor glanced over at me before he turned back to Fabien with his usual blank expression. He crossed his arms, waiting for an explanation.

As the general sang his own praises, he barely paused for breath, which, admittedly, impressed me. "As you can see, my prince, the war is won. I have captured the enemy's leader, and after his people hear that he is dead, they will surren—"

"So you mean to tell me that you take credit for all this?" Alastor interrupted him, gesturing in my direction.

"Yes, it was I who captured this traitor, after all," Fabien boasted, his chest puffing up with pride.

"I see." Alastor stepped closer. It appeared he and the general had a different understanding of the circumstances leading to my imprisonment. "I

26

was wondering which one of my generals would be daft enough to defy a direct order from me."

Fabien's eyes widened.

I assumed he thought capturing me would bring yields of personal glory to him. I stifled my laugh when I saw him start to panic. "Prince Alastor, but I—"

"Did I or did I not order you to move your troops to the side of Heimdall City?"

Fabien lowered his head. "You did, sir."

"Where did you move your troops, then?" Alastor asked.

"Back to our nearest fort."

If it weren't for my current circumstances, I would've laughed at the way General Fabien wilted under a few questions from Alastor who, I came to realize, had that effect on most people. In a game of cards, it was said Alastor always had a full hand, and even if he didn't, his opponents didn't have a chance.

When Alastor spoke again, he threw down his ace. "Let me remind you, Fabien. You can let that hubris of yours cloud your eyes and make you delusional, but don't you forget that I have countless qualified and talented generals that are craving to take your place. I have no greater need for Archer as my prisoner than I do for you as my general. Understood?"

Fabien stared back in both fear and outrage. The anger, however, only seemed to dig Fabien into a deeper grave. "I don't know what our King was thinking when he appointed you as the crown prince. Under Prince Fallon, I won countless battles. You're wasting my potential if you let me go."

Alastor laughed humorlessly. "Which battles? The ones against the escaping sheep in our farm cities? That was by far the most impressive account in your portfolio, I must say."

Fabien stormed out without another word. He slammed the door shut behind him.

"Pathetic," Alastor muttered at the exact same time as I did. As if my voice reminded him of my presence, Alastor turned to me. "I have a feeling that we've been here before."

I sighed. "And I have a feeling you won't let me go this time."

Alastor scoffed but didn't respond immediately. "Do you know what I think of this war, Archer?"

"That it was doomed for us to begin with?"

"No. I thought that it was nothing more than foolishness. Heimdall City was already destined to fall. The faeries would kill each other over matters of survival."

"I'm a faerie too, if you weren't aware." Though I wouldn't admit it, I knew he was right.

He held my gaze in a challenge. "So you know it firsthand. Tell me, Archer. How many friendships have been ruined in the city? How many families have been torn apart?"

I remained silent, which he took as an answer.

"War is always meant to be a last resort. I don't believe that this is the case here," Alastor said softly. For a second, the expression on his face slipped into one of longing and sadness. It was gone in the next instant.

"Then why are you fighting? Why waste so much blood over a cause that you don't believe in?"

"If it were up to me, I wouldn't. I don't even understand this whole faerie and fairy thing. But, of course, I'm not the one in full control here." He turned back to face me, a small smile flitting across his face. "But that doesn't mean I can't do something about it."

I stared at him, a little surprised to hear this from the Crown Prince. "What are you planning? May I help?"

"I'm not quite done with my idea. But when the time comes, I will need your help."

"I'd be more than willing."

He nodded. "Let's go then. If you keep to the east side of the camp, you'll make it out without being seen. I'll order the guards to switch. You won't have to deal with anyone on your way out."

"So, you're letting me go after all?"

He smiled. "I did say that you were of no use to me as a prisoner, did I?"

"Ouch. I'd like to think that I have my uses, prisoner or not. I have to say, that hurt a little."

"Did it, now?" Just like the last time I met him, I could hear the amusement in his voice.

"You could win the war with me."

Alastor shook his head, his smirk fading. "I wouldn't be so sure. If I were to kill you here, yes, it would demoralize the faeries. But I doubt they'd give up so easily. Not when they have a purpose to fight for and a martyr to honor."

I felt a spark of pride igniting inside of me at his words. The realization that I helped my people recognize their worth hit me hard. I was so distracted in that gentle, glimmering feeling that I almost didn't notice Alastor leaving the room.

"Goodbye for now, Alastor," I felt compelled to say before he left.

He glanced at me over his shoulder. "Goodbye, and good luck, Archer."

I realized here and now that this could be the beginning of the end. The faeries may have been fighting a losing war, but perhaps my alliance with Alastor would be enough to turn the tides. Maybe, just maybe, it would be the fighting chance that we had all dreamed of.

TORRENTIAL EVENTS
by Ethan Ho

Volcanoes

Pyroclastic, Vehement

Exploding, Expanding, Erupting

Rocks, Lava, Cliffs, Ash

Blowing, Weathering, Eroding

Charred, Discolored

Plateaus

Tornado

Turbulent, Violent

Spiraling, Spinning, Swirling

Whirlwinds, Tempest, Maelstrom, Whirlpools

Churning, Brewing, Revolving

Consuming, Inescapable

Vortex

WHERE I'M FROM

by Hailey Zuniga

I'm from all the places I've learned to embrace.

I'm from sandy beaches with the scorching sun.

I'm from the people who've said your life has only just begun.

I'm from a group of friends who I know will never last.

I'm from a family of writers whose standards hold me higher.

I'm from a "bad" generation that has many obligations,

But it doesn't define who I'll be or who I am.

DEAR AMMIE

by Audrey Pham

DEAR AMMIE,

I'M GOING TO DIE. It won't be anything dramatic, or bloody, or heroic. And I'm not a part of any gang or drug cartel. I won't be murdered in the dead of the night from my windowsill or in any other grisly event. In fact, I'd be better off with that being the case. It's too humiliating to admit what everybody else knows about me, that I'll die of old age and loneliness. I suppose it hurts far too much to say that I'm not the girl or woman that I once was.

Seventy-three sounded young to me. *I'm going to live forever*, I told your father. I swore that I would be a cranky old bat for my great-grandchildren. Ninety-six was the youngest I'd settle for. I wanted to explore the world, even if it was from the rocking chair in front of our old beach house. In response, he told me, *Nobody deserves such a horrible fate*. You know George had a terrible sense of humor. At least my death would give me a chance to get a joke of my own over him, just this once.

I know you won't tell anybody about this letter because you're ashamed of me. I know you'll deny it because you want to be a good daughter. But the thing is, Ammie, you already are. If your own mother can't understand you inside and out, whoever will? If you're embarrassed by me, I get it—hell, I would be too if my mother pretended to have Alzheimer's at Thanksgiving so that everyone would leave her be. I'm sure I'm not the first one to tell you that I've lost myself a little after your father died.

Amelia Marie Veloni, don't cry because I used *that* word. Saying somebody "passed away" is too misleading. Your father would have wanted us to say things as they were, and I don't want you telling everybody that your senile mother "passed away" or "left us." Tell it as it is. That's my last request.

You're also wondering why I wrote this letter for you. Have I really lost it this time? Am I still pretending that I have a mental illness? No, my dear Ammie. Amidst all the rambling, this letter is simply an old woman trying to let her daughter know that she loves her very much. That's what us Velonis all have in common: we aren't comfortable with expressing our feelings.

I'd say I'd rather die than let you know I'm going to end this letter because I'm about to cry—but that would have already happened. So I suppose there's no harm in telling you.

Love you, forever and always,

Ma

LIVE LIKE LEGENDS

by Teresa Le

Born into a family,

Raised into adulthood,

Not knowing what's next.

We graduate from school after eighteen years,

Our life begins and we take flight—

As seniors, they say our futures are bright.

Your father's pride, your mother's joy,

Those memories of playing with your toys,

And all those other childish ploys.

To learning how to make wrongs right,

To trying and fighting to find your own light.

But no matter where you've gone,

You've made your mark,

From pen and paper to the love in someone's heart.

Inspired by legends like Lincoln and Washington

To live, encourage, and lead others.

You may not be president, but you can open those doors

As a doctor, an author, or maybe even more.

To someone else, you've lived their dream.

You don't have to be famous;

You're already living the life of legends.

FRAGMENTS

by Teresa Le

I remember how you came to me,
Hopeless eyes, a shattered life,
Seeking to be set free.

You cracked me, piece by piece
To fill in every hole in your heart.

Then you left me broken,
As torn as you were
When you first came to me.

If only you saw the
Fragments I am now
And pieced *me* back together, too.

IN PLAIN SIGHT

by Audrey Pham

JOURNAL ENTRY NUMBER 74: My name is Jackson. I'm fourteen years old, fifteen this March. I like bird-watching, Philly cheesesteak sandwiches, and football.

Also, my best friend is invisible.

When I tell people about Clark, they think I'm crazy or stupid. But Clark is real.

He was physically solid up until he was thirteen. Always a scrawny little thing, about two heads shorter than me, and he still wears the thickest glasses ever, but he's the coolest guy I know.

I'm grateful he still needs to wear glasses. Comes in handy along with his invisibility. Sometimes, when people make fun of me, they start screaming after seeing a pair of glasses hanging mid-air.

He scared my mom a whole lot, too, but she's used to him now. She really loves Clark, maybe even more so after he became invisible. Mom calls him a "science-defying phenomenon" and other things like that.

She's reading over my shoulder right now as I'm writing in my journal, and she's telling me I should write about *how* Clark became invisible. Or maybe the time when I discovered he was actually invisible.

Fine, I tell her, so she leaves my room. But her suggestion got me thinking.

It was about two years ago. I remember it was around five in the morning when I heard sharp taps at my window.

Who the heck could be awake at this time? I thought it was either my imagination or the wind, so I tried to go back to sleep.

I heard more noise a few minutes later, and I nearly screamed.

The window was all the way open. Somebody had broken in.

"Clark," I yelled in spite of my fear. On the off-chance it was actually him, since this wouldn't be the first time he's snuck into my room, I didn't want to make a bigger fool out of myself by falling for his prank. "Stop messing with me. I know it's you."

"Damn it," he muttered. "How'd you know it was me?"

Relief flooded my senses. "Seems like something dumb you would do."

I turned on the light. I wasn't even mad that he had broken in, that's how relieved I was. I'd surely be dead if an intruder had gotten through my window, and also if it got on the news. *"Utah Boy Couldn't Stop a Burglar When He Had the Chance!"*

"What are you doing here so early?" I started searching for him, and that was when I realized something was wrong.

Clark was nowhere to be seen.

I looked under my bed because that was where he liked to hide sometimes since he was so small. But all that was there was some dirty laundry and old books.

"Clark?" I called out. "Did you leave already?"

"Nah," he said. "Still here."

"What?" I looked around again. "Where are you?"

"I'm right next to you." I could feel his warm breath in my face. My heart skipped a beat when I saw his thick glasses hanging next to my ear.

"No you're not," I whispered. My hands began to shake, and I had an urge to scream and cry at the same time. "I can't see you at all."

He sighed. "I forgot. I'm invisible now."

"This isn't funny, Clark. What happened?" I tried sounding serious and angry, but all I felt was confused and scared. I thought maybe I was still sleeping and this was some twisted nightmare.

37

If I could see him, he would probably roll his eyes. "I told you," he repeated. "I'm invisible now. Dad says he can save a lot of money on tickets at the movies and at amusement parks, but we can't eat out anymore. It's not all that bad, though. I was outside scaring Hyde and Jason. I have a killer dead-person voice."

My shaking got worse, and tears spilled from my eyes. I blinked hard to keep them at bay. My heartbeat was so loud in my ears that I swore even Clark could hear it, so I looked the other way to try and save my dignity. I desperately wanted to lie back down with my blanket over my head in an attempt to pretend it was all a dream that I could bring up and laugh about with Clark later.

Instead, I sat there, trembling, in front of my best friend who no longer existed.

"I know it's hard to believe," he said. "I couldn't understand it either at first. I thought I died and this was me, my ghost. That's what my parents thought, too. But no. I feel pretty real."

"I don't believe you."

"Ask my parents then. They won't tell anyone, but they'll tell you."

"What happened?"

Even though I couldn't see it, I could feel him shrug.

The words fell out of my mouth, hushed and horrified, "God. You're like a monster now or something."

Despite everything, Clark burst out into laughter. "'Or something.' Dude, why are you so freaked out? It's not like I'm Dracula and I just sunk my teeth into your neck."

He kept on laughing to the point of hiccupping, as if being invisible was nothing unusual.

I stopped shaking, and found myself clutching my stomach because of how hard I was laughing along with him. I didn't know when the crying stopped and the laughing started. That's what you would do, too, if your friend was invisible.

Mom pounded on my door. "Jackson," she whispered angrily. "How is this entire house supposed to sleep with you laughing like a madman?"

"My fault, Mrs. Devoll," Clark called out. "I woke him up."

Startled upon recognizing the voice, Mom asked, "Clark? When did you come over?" She opened my door. "Where are you?"

I sighed, and if he were still real, we would've made eye contact and given each other the exact same look. "Clark can tell you everything, Mom."

FORGETFULNESS

by Hailey Zuniga

Forgetting comes naturally,

But it scares me.

I don't want to forget these memories.

I don't want to forget the way you hold me,

Or the way you say my name.

I don't want to forget the way you shine like the sun,

Or your unwavering patience.

I know forgetfulness will never come

As long as you're here with me.

THE BRIDE AND THE BRIMSTONE
by Kevin Nguyen

Is marriage love or a bind?
Some winding ball and chain?
The bride has made her decision
And cannot sense the pain.

She wanders down the gates, completely unaware;
Demons wave at her arrival,
Burnt flowers scatter across the air.
The groom tugs at his collar, bothered by the flames.
The priest bares his teeth and calls out both their names.

He lends his hand as she makes her way up the steps.
She, of course, takes it,
But is not ready to forget.
The priest clears his throat, announces the proposal:
"To abandon the past, and nevermore feel woeful."

But the fallen angel, observing atop his throne,
Cries out in laughter—and dooms them to be alone.

FOR I HAVE SINNED

by Jessica Truong

"BLESS ME, FATHER, for I have sinned," Agnis whispers, her palms clammy. "My last confession was two years ago."

She's a good kid, so much so that there's no need to confess her sins to the vessel of God, but here she is with strands of hair sticking to her forehead and eyes bloodshot from spending days indoors, withering away in the home that used to house two people.

"I killed someone," she confesses, the words falling out bitter and dry as ash. "I don't know what to do with the body."

Her hands are clasped into a desperate prayer to the Lord. She repents in the safe veil of anonymity inside the confession booth, for the Bible says that all sins can be forgiven. She's young, far too young to be worrying about her place in heaven, but the crime she's committed would have her dragged, kicking and screaming, to the devil.

"My boyfriend," she clarifies. There is silence from the priest, her own hushed voice loud in her ears. "I killed him. I smashed his head in with a lamp."

Agnis takes a breath, shaky and slow. "He was mine for a year after high school. We were in love. He'd put his varsity jacket over my shoulders in the hallway, and I'd come watch his games." She laughs a little. "We were really happy in senior year, then we both went to the same university."

The silver cross strung around her neck itches. It feels dirty to wear the Lord's symbol now. She can't bear to look at the priest even through the

42

diamond pattern that obscures her face from him. Instead, she stares at the scratched carving on the varnished wood inside the booth, a crude mark made from insolent teenagers that are just as careless and rambunctious as she was.

In retrospect, Agnis can only sit through their final week together, picking apart each and every sign that their relationship wasn't meant to be, but no one expects to murder their loved one in cold blood.

* * *

In the days leading up, the stars seemed to have aligned, piling misfortune onto them. Their love was one of playful innocence and embarrassed glances towards one another in what could only be described as a suspended honeymoon phase. Snarky conversations here and there weren't anything to raise eyebrows at; it was when the spark faded, when someone saw their loved one next to them on the sofa in their most vulnerable state, and there was no urge to smother them in love.

It was Wednesday. The heater was broken, an unpleasant start to the chill of winter.

"Kye," Agnis called out, bundled in a coat and blankets. "Can you see what's wrong with the heater? There's no hot air coming in."

Kye poked his head in, donning a woolen beanie that made his dark curls stick out from underneath. He, too, was waddling around in thick sweaters and scarves. "I don't know how to fix heaters."

She scrunched up her face. "Can't you just check?"

He gave her a cheeky smile that made his dimples appear. "I will if you come with me."

She agreed, albeit reluctantly, before she layered on another pair of sweatpants to trudge through the thick snow piling up on the soft, damp dirt that Massachusetts was so eager to provide. There were no neighbors foolish enough to step out into the snow, and the streets, for once, were devoid of life.

In the white mist of nothingness, Kye's dark hair and patterned attire made her bury her face into her scarf to hide the lovestruck smile on her lips.

The heater was not fixed, just as they had originally expected, and after Kye's final attempt at fixing the wiring followed by a loud curse, they ran back inside in a bout of laughter and half-hearted shoves, warmed enough by each other's presence.

* * *

Agnis did not have blonde hair. Kye did not have blond hair either.

She doesn't remember much about that day, only that it was like no other, and that's why it still scared her.

Flashes of anger and resentment were what drove her to grab the nearest thing to her. Maybe it was Kye's inability to explain why there was blonde hair stuck in a hairbrush she never owned. Maybe it was the way he avoided eye contact with her, a tell-tale sign of him lying which she picked up on from how long they'd been together. It was even the way he couldn't get a believable lie out that made her see red.

In the growing pool of blood seeping into the cold wood floor, white and blue ceramic shards scattered like a grotesque mosaic. What was left of the lamp lay next to Kye's limp head, and damp curls stuck to his forehead.

Agnis's heart beat quick and fast, pounding in her ears so loudly that she was afraid neighbors would come knocking to ask about the noise.

"I didn't mean to," she whispered to nobody. Maybe she was whispering to the corpse on the ground, maybe she wasn't, but whoever she was attempting to convince did not respond. "I didn't mean to. I was just angry." Her body shook as she tried to shake his. "Please wake up."

Agnis was a name that meant "pure and holy," but she felt like neither of those things as her fingertips dipped into the thick blood to drag her boyfriend's prone form into her lap. She cradled his head, leaning down and picking the shards embedded into his scalp, the smell of iron overwhelming and suffocating. His eyes were still open, unfocused and listless—he stared past her, past the living world.

"I'm sorry," she said helplessly, but an apology was no good when the boyfriend she was apologizing to was bleeding out on the floor. "I'm sorry."

* * *

In the moment of silence following her confession, Agnis rests her head against the wooden walls and closes her eyes. She opens them again when the man on the other side speaks in a low, somber tone.

"My dear, do you truly regret this act?" the priest asks. It is earnest and unlike the confident, soaring voice of the ambassador of God; he sounds like a soft-spoken old man, subject to the second-hand guilt of keeping a young man's murder under an oath of secrecy.

A beat. Then—

"Yes." She sounds breathless, relieved.

The confession follows the same rhythm as any other does, a surprisingly monotonous routine that she scrapes to find solace in.

Although her sins are forgiven in the eyes of the Church, the heavy lump of guilt stays settled in her stomach when she returns home and steps over the same place she was on her hands and knees, scrubbing every crevice of the hardwood floor.

And it stays settled there when she thinks of her boyfriend buried under layers of snow and dirt miles away, along with the blonde hair and hairbrush.

45

FNET = MA

by Tracy Vo

The problem states we've got a block
Sliding across the table it's on.
It asks that after it's slowed down and stopped,
How far would the block have gone?

Now we've got a block on the ground,
Accelerating to the right.
There's no movement up or down,
But all forces are still in sight.

What should we do first?
"Draw a free-body diagram."
Do it just as we rehearsed,
Always use one on the AP exam.

What directions do you pick? Go on, discuss.
"Down and left is minus, up and right is plus."
What else do we have? Shout it in reply,
"There is no acceleration in the y."

Force of gravity goes down, it's minus mg.
Normal force points up, they're equal, you see?
Remember to keep the direction in mind,
Add those vectors, they're zero combined.

Write down your equation,
It's Newton's 2nd Law.
Fnet equals mass times acceleration,
Move on, you've almost finished it all.

From here it's just your skills in math,
Substitute letters and solve for the unknown.
The best approach is the simplest path,
Remember to check that your work is shown.

Now that the problem is over
And you've had your fun,
Make sure there's nothing left to cover.
That's it, you're finally done!

THE GEODE
by Kevin Le

Chalcedony

A rough outer shield;
A thousand angels. Darlings
Won't you shelter me?

Quartz

Sweet, milky ichor
Seemingly frail yet sturdy
Dark until opened

Crystals

Oh, shiny diamonds
Flaunt your beauty to the world
Yet dimly, dimly

OH, HOW THE MIGHTY FALL
by Kellan Nguyen

"GWENDOLYN, WHAT ARE YOU DOING?"

The archangel jolts up, her navy robes and wings startling with the motion, and she drags her gaze away from the scenery below the clouds. She leans away from the balcony railings and smiles sheepishly at her twin brother Gwen, who looks on with crossed arms and narrowed eyes. "Nothing."

Not again. Gwen smiles back despite himself.

It's a familiar song and dance they share; he and his sister carry out their barrage of heavenly duties, she rushes to finish early, and once everything is said and done for the day, he finds her leaning over the golden railings of Paradisum, staring at the Earth below—wistful glances that last too long.

"You're lucky I'm the one who always catches you," he says. "Imagine if Pac or the other knights caught you staring at the humans. Or, Paradisum forbid, the High Gods themselves." He shivers at the thought.

Gwendolyn shrugs. "It's not like Celeste or Celdic can stop me. It's my job to watch over the planets."

"Yes, *all* the planets."

She takes one last glance at Earth below before she turns to stroll down the pearly white brick road, her lavender hair and navy robes billowing in the ever-present breeze.

Close at her heels, Gwen lowers his voice. "Still, though, you shouldn't be looking at the humans like that all the time. The knights will catch you eventually, and Celeste or Celdic might ban you outright."

"Relax, Gwen, we're archangels. The knights can't do anything to us, even if they're under Celeste's command."

"But the Gods themselves still can." He grimaces. "Humans surely aren't worth suffering divine punishment." He nearly runs into her back when she stops walking.

She whirls around to face him, brows furrowed. "But they are. Celeste put you in charge of watching stars, not planets and moons, so you wouldn't understand."

And she's right, he doesn't. He doesn't understand what all the fuss is about humanity no matter how many times he catches her gazing down at them more often than her job of documenting planets entails. Even though he and his sister share the same opinions on everything else, this remains their sole point of contention.

He raises his hands up in surrender and attempts to smile. Before he can get a word out, she stomps up the stairs to the archives building where all scribes store their observations.

"I'm going to get started on tomorrow's work now," she says. "You can join me."

"Doing extra work out of the goodness of your heart?"

She turns back to him and her grin returns. "Of course." Before the door closes behind her, she says, "Remember, don't tell anyone."

And then she's gone without waiting for an answer. He rolls his eyes. There is nothing that needs to be said, after all; the sky would fall sooner than he'd betray her, and he knows that sentiment is returned.

* * *

"And did you know they've only just discovered the concept of space-time? Isn't that adorable?" Gwendolyn says.

No one else is around this early, so Gwen slumps over the polished

50

tabletop of the Central Paradisian Library, and his wings droop.

"Gwendolyn, please," he says. "You've mentioned it about a dozen times now. And it wasn't recent, that was a century ago for them."

She smiles in response, bright and toothy, the reflected stars in her eyes dancing. "But you have to admit they're pretty charming."

"Yes," he says, "but in that way you laugh at a fledgling's foolish mistakes."

She has the gall to laugh as if he's made a joke. Then, she reaches over to one of the many towers of books stacked next to her and pulls out a thick, cloth-bound text. "Here's my favorite one. It's not a record written by any of my angels, but something the humans wrote. The *humans,* Gwen." She flips through it and stops near the middle. "Just look."

He absently scans through the foreign characters and sits upright when he finally registers what it is. "Literature? They allow this here?"

"Of course." Gwendolyn flips through the unevenly cut pages. "I assume it's for just archival purposes, but I've rarely seen any mortal novels documented. It's mostly literature from our sister galaxies."

He shrugs in response, reading bits and pieces he sees between Gwendolyn's arbitrary skimming. "Wait, stop here." He takes the book into his hands. Time disappears as he loses himself in lines of prose, the words flowing with a certain rhythm he can't fully understand but feels drawn to. He doesn't notice how far he is until he flips the page only to find the back cover.

Over the top edge of the book, Gwendolyn gives him a look. "You enjoyed it, didn't you?"

"Nonsense."

She grabs another novel off a stack. "We can read this one together. I haven't gone through it yet."

They make a habit out of it. Gwen continues to train scouts to help him map the endless space Celeste oversees and Gwendolyn keeps up with her scribe duties, but early in the day, before regular Paradisians are supposed to wake up, they sit together in the library, tearing through novel after novel. A voice in his head warns him that Celeste could find out about this, but he can't help himself.

Eventually, they run out because all things come to an end. The final book they read is apparently what humans consider a classic: something about a man put on trial for an unknown crime. It draws to a close in tragedy, a punishment that may or may not have been justified. Gwen closes the book in contemplative silence. He had lost track of time, so he startles when the library door opens with a click and other angels flood in, ready to get to start their day.

Wordlessly, Gwen and his sister drift outside, past the stream of angels, and stop near the railings behind the complex that overlooks Earth. This is where he has caught her standing, listless and alone, time and time again, and today he joins her. The waves of Earth's cerulean sea below pale in comparison to Paradisum's glittering indigoes and royal golds, but he supposes they're beautiful in their own way.

"Why do you like humans so much?" The words slip out before he can stop them. "Why risk everything?"

She tilts her head towards the sky. "You've read their books with me. You know what they're capable of creating."

"But we can do the same."

"Exactly," she says and looks back down at Earth. "They're so small, you know? They haven't even been outside of their solar system, let alone other galaxies. But they can do so much. They're weak, but they try." She purses her lips. "That's more than what can be said about some of us here. And they're so free. The Gods don't tell them what to do. They can go wherever they want."

Gwen still doesn't understand why that's so important, and a flare of frustration wells up but fizzles out as quickly as it came. He wants to reassure her, wants to say something like how Paradisum is just as good as Earth, if not better, but even if he could bring himself to speak, the words would fall flat.

He doesn't need to say anything, though, because someone else does: "What are you two doing?"

In sync, Gwen and Gwendolyn whirl around to see a knight land on the clean white bricks, wings folding closed, the metal of his engraved chestplate gleaming in the daylight.

Before Gwen can make up an excuse, his sister crosses her arms. "What's it to you?"

If not for billions of years practicing proper etiquette, Gwen's jaw would've dropped open, but he reins himself in.

His sister continues, "Can't an archangel relax in the peace of the heavens?"

The knight—Pac, Gwen thinks his name is—doesn't seem to take offense to Gwendolyn's words, and if he does, he's professional enough to not show it. "Is it not time for the archangels to begin their duties?" He inclines his head. "Celeste will know. She always does."

Whether he's referring to people-watching or neglect of heavenly duties, Gwen isn't sure. Before his sister can speak again, Gwen says, "There's no reason for Celeste to be concerned. We were simply admiring the view before going about the day. Nothing to be worried about."

"And if there *was* something to report," Gwendolyn adds, "she wouldn't be concerned with me being such a diligent worker, would she?"

Pac hums noncommittedly, neither a reprimand nor an agreement. "Regardless, you best get to work." With that, he turns around to return to his patrol, wings spread out. "And remember," he says over his shoulder, "Celeste is always watching."

This time, it's Gwendolyn who sneaks up on him instead of the other way around. He's in the main conference room giving his fledgling scouts their assignments for the week when she appears in a shower of stardust. "Gwen, you will *not* believe what just—oh, sorry."

Despite her words, she doesn't sound very sorry. He sighs and lists the remaining assignments before waving his subordinates away. "You're lucky I was almost finished with them anyway. What's got you so excited?"

Gwendolyn grins ear to ear, bouncing on the balls of her feet, the most emotion she's shown in public in a millennium. "Celeste was busy, so I—"

"So, you did what?"

"She had a meeting somewhere or she was with Celdic or something, I don't know. As I was saying, she was gone, so I had the chance to go down to Earth—"

"You *what?*"

"Stop interrupting me." She huffs and crosses her arms, but uncrosses them in the very next moment to gesture wildly. "Humans are so amazing, Gwen. They're nothing at all like I imagined. They're more, so much more. I can't even begin to describe them."

Gwen feels his energy drain. "Gwendolyn …"

Likewise, she mellows out. "I know." She lowers her hands to her side. "The knights will catch me if I go down again, and Celeste might even call me up personally. But it's worth it. They're worth it."

For the first time he can remember, the silence is stifling. The gap between them widens.

He becomes hyperaware of the room they're in, and the blinding white walls and tall windows make him feel like throwing up. He should never feel like this, he thinks, because he's not supposed to.

An emptiness wells up inside him. "Okay."

She blinks. "Okay?"

"I trust you," he says, but the weight is still not gone. "Besides, you wouldn't listen to me if I warned you, right?"

Her narrowed, starry eyes pierce through him. "I wouldn't." She doesn't hide the disappointment in her voice when she says, "Come with me next time, Gwen."

He doesn't have to give an answer; he's sure she knows what it is anyway.

* * *

As the months pass, Celeste's absences become more common and so do Gwendolyn's descents into the mortal realm. Gwen catches her staring down at Earth more often than before, wisps of melancholy on her face instead of her former awe and wonder. He loses himself in the work of his scouts in an effort to distract himself from this version of his sister while she, in turn, spends less time in the archives.

Without fail, however, she always tells him about her latest adventures on Earth. She tells him of long stretches of sand, beaches of sea glass, and lakes of deep blues and seafoam greens. She tells tales of mountain ranges that humans have trekked across and drawn on their primitive maps, of quiet countryside towns and bustling cities that never seem to sleep. And she tells him of the mortal, the human boy who shows her everything.

At that point, Gwen blanks out, and the realization hits him: she's growing attached. What he thought was a passing interest has grown into more, and it terrifies him because who knows what could happen if anyone else found out? Gwendolyn is stealthy enough in her escapades, but what will she do if a knight catches her leaving, if Celeste does?

Gwen doesn't have an answer, and he doesn't want one. His sister certainly won't stop descending, and he knows it will all catch up to her. It's only a matter of time.

Today, Celeste is gone again, and that can only mean one thing. He hasn't lost his sister yet, but he feels the pang of her absence all the same.

* * *

Gwen doesn't know how it happens, but he feels the aftershocks echo throughout the heavens. "Have you heard?" a passerby mutters to their friend. "An angel fled today."

He's on his way to the archives as usual, but that makes him stop in his tracks. He almost turns around to interrogate those two angels, but they're already gone, walking several paces away, and deep down, he already knows which angel has left.

For confirmation's sake, he rushes to the archives.

Sure enough, an empty building is all that greets him. There's not even a regular scribe in sight, presumably gone for the knights to take attendance of who's left. The place is just a shell of itself and he finds nobody here, so he heads back towards where he knows a crowd is congregating near the Paradisian Gates. Bits and pieces of conversation come to him all at once.

"—one of the scribes—"

"—the archangel—"

"—knights chased them—"

"—an actual archangel?"

"—descended—"

"—jumped down—"

"—can you believe—"

"—Earth, of all places—"

He closes his eyes, tunes everything out. He's heard enough. One of his scouts will eventually come to him with the official status report, but for now, it's enough.

* * *

Against the blinding white backdrop of her office, Celeste looks the same as she did billions of years ago, curly hair like nebulae flowing around her like a halo, white robes crisp and pristine. Her galaxy eyes bore into Gwen's entire skull, and it takes all his self-restraint to not flinch and look away. Even as an archangel, the supposed right-hand of the High Gods, there's a chilling distance between them that's all the more apparent when he's in her presence.

When she speaks, it's like space curls in on itself to accommodate her. "You must be wondering why I called you here personally."

His fingertips dig into the plush chair across from her. "I would never begin to think about questioning you or your will."

"None of that, archangel." She waves her hand in a dismissive gesture, eyes falling closed, and Gwen feels like he can breathe again. "There's no need for formalities."

"So why did you call me in?"

Celeste is silent for several dreadful moments before she says, "Do you know what your sister has been up to?"

"Can you elaborate?"

She leans in. "I have been absent in Paradisum as of late, and it's been brought to my attention that a certain archangel has taken advantage of that."

Gwen is good at masking his emotions, it's what angels like him have to do, but all of that melts away in front of the God of Space herself.

"Don't worry your little head," Celeste says. "I know you have nothing to do with it, even if you *are* siblings."

There's a flash of something in her eyes for the briefest moment, but Gwen can't decipher it. "What worries me is what I do know: your sister has been lax in her duties. I thought it was a phase at first, because who dares go against my wishes, right?" She sighs, fake and mocking. "Sadly, I was wrong, and it appears my little angel has truly abandoned me."

Gwen swallows. "What do you want me to do about this?"

She smiles, and every muscle in his body tenses. "Your mission, second archangel Gwen, is to find the first archangel Gwendolyn and bring her to me. Even if it means dragging her back kicking and screaming."

* * *

After billions of years spent together, it isn't hard to find his sister again.

He finds her on a beach with the human. Free from those stuffy Paradisian robes he knows she hates, instead clad in a simple, white dress. Openly laughing. Happier than she'd ever been before, even when they were young. When she notices his presence, it's like someone turns her off, and she tugs the human behind her like she used to do with Gwen when they were little.

The first thing he says is, "Why?"

She stares at him for a long, long time, and waves for the human to walk away without breaking eye contact. "I wanted to be free, Gwen," she says, and something akin to anger, unbridled and unfamiliar, boils over in him.

"You—you can't just leave like that!" His wings, once perpetually tucked away, flare out. "Just because you wanted something, wanted that single little thing, doesn't mean you can abandon everything. Did you even think about your angels? Your home?" *Me?*

"Oh my Gods," she yells out, raising her voice for the first time. "Have you ever listened to me? Paid attention? Did you ever notice how I really felt, or did all those times you caught me mean nothing beyond the surface? I was miserable, Gwen." She lets out a short laugh. "I was right when I said it back then: you really don't understand."

"Then explain it to me. Don't just leave and drop everything all of a sudden."

"I've been trying," she says right back, "for so long. I got you to read everything they wrote, we watched them together, I literally told you the reason why I love them so much. And you were there every time I came back. Every single time. What's there not to understand, Gwen?"

He doesn't know what to say to that, because no matter what she tells him, he will never understand it the way she does. "Did you even like being an angel, at least?"

"Yes. Once upon a time, I really was happy up there." She glances up at where Paradisum always looks down. "Not now, though. I don't think I've been happy up there for a long time."

Another topic in which they diverge, another point of contention that widens the gap between them. Gwen doesn't know if happiness is what he feels in Paradisum, but he does know he would rather live up there than down on Earth. "Why else did you leave, then? Besides the humans."

Gwendolyn smiles, a small but sure thing. "I'm selfish. I truly am. I couldn't spend another minute up there after billions of years trapped in it." She pauses. "I was going to tell you. About me leaving."

"Were you really?"

She nods and says, "Of course. I was in the middle of leaving you a note right before I left, but then the knights found me, and … you know the story."

All the fight drains out of him. He doesn't think he was truly angry in the first place, anyway. He couldn't stand to be. "I don't want you to just—to just leave like this."

"You can come with me, Gwen," she says, and it's like a dam in him breaks, bursts open, and he feels emptier than ever. "Please. We can be free, away from all that Paradisum nonsense. We can do whatever we want, go wherever we want, and nobody can breathe down our necks or police us. We can be truly happy, Gwen."

He doesn't cry. He refuses to. But he comes close, and he knows

59

Gwendolyn has seen the tense slope of his shoulders, the ugly way his face scrunches up to keep the tears from falling. She steps closer, steadily, like she's approaching a wounded animal. It's terrible.

"Celeste told me to bring you back," he finally says.

"Oh." She shifts from foot to foot, and it reminds Gwen of their younger years. "So what are you going to do?"

"You already know the answer."

Gwendolyn smiles, big and bright and so very sad. "I do. I guess this means goodbye, doesn't it?" She closes the distance between them and sweeps him up in a crushing hug. Gwen doesn't know if he hugs her back or not. Celeste will find out what he's done, she always does, but for now, everything falls away. He feels impossibly more lost.

"Just go," Gwen says, but it's him that leaves. It's him who pulls back, turns away, it's him who can't bear to look back, and he knows this is the last time he'll ever see his sister.

* * *

The end of the world starts with a whisper: *the Paradisian Gates have been sealed shut.* All around him, scribes and scouts break out in a frenzy, and loud mutterings and exclamations pile atop one another. Beyond all of it, every Paradisian comes to a conclusion: something is wrong.

And then the scribes' cries split the air, because underneath the gold-threaded clouds and grandiose city of the heavens, the Earth is dying. Vast, blue oceans run red with blood, and explosions ripple through the ground. Plumes of smoke spill into the atmosphere with deadly speed, and it won't be long until they cover the entire surface of the planet.

The knights try to maintain a semblance of order, but it all comes crashing down as a loud crack echoes through all of Paradisum. It's followed by smaller cracks that spread beneath the angels' feet and creep up the sides of towering marble buildings. They don't fall immediately, but crumble more and more every passing second until a fragment of stone falls out, and another one, and a larger chunk, and then the whole wall falls apart after billions of years standing proud.

Many yell out in shock, some in anger, and a few call out for the High Gods to provide an explanation. Nobody seems particularly scared. They're immortals, after all, created for the sole purpose of serving a higher being.

Then the first ray of light beams down on someone, and as soon as the light disappears, the angel standing there disappears as well. No ash, no fire and brimstone. Just a flash of light, and they're gone. More flashes of light appear, and the panic finally begins. There are screams, and there are more cries for Celeste as if this disaster will lure her out.

Gwen watches from a nook in the clouds above. He registers all of this distantly; it doesn't feel real, this supposed end of the universe. But here it is, looking him right in the face, daring him to think otherwise. It's strange, he thinks. The end of the world doesn't come in some great, climactic battle. It comes in waves.

His emotions, too, come in waves. He watches as Paradisum, the only place he's known, crumbles into nothingness when the disbelief hits him. Then comes shock and denial, despair, and a deep rage he's never felt before.

Celeste is the reason behind all of this, he realizes. She must be, because no calamity like this could ever befall Paradisum if it wasn't her will. There's a reason why she turns a blind eye and deaf ear to the hundreds of thousands of her own angels who are crying out for her, blinking out of existence. But there's still the question of why she's doing it.

The memories come back to him: her absences, Gwendolyn's escapades, the suspicious timing of it all.

He stands up. He needs to find his sister.

Celeste is not in her office when Gwen bursts in. Instead, he finds someone else. "What did you do? Where is she?"

The High God of Time, Celdic, smirks from where he sits behind the desk, as if he's been expecting Gwen's arrival. "Awfully bold of you to assume your little sister is worth any trouble," Celdic says, lilting voice more irritating than ever.

"Answer my question."

Celdic stands up and leans forward, hands braced on the table. The smirk sharpens into something more dangerous. "What makes you think you can talk to me that way?" Gwen clenches his fist. "Celeste is delivering divine punishment, that's all."

"Punishment?" Gwen echoes. "For what?" But he already knows the answer.

Celdic must know that he knows, too, because his lips curl up further and Gwen feels the same fight-or-flight instinct he had when Celeste smiled at him. "Poor little archangel Gwendolyn," he says, "always sneaking off to watch the humans, to be with them as if she could just shed her wings and become the perfect mortal." He shakes his head and tuts. "Didn't she know her place as an archangel, one of Celeste's own creations? Instead of being up in Paradisum, she left you all to become human, of all things. Choosing humanity over divinity? There's only one answer, and she chose wrong."

"She didn't. It's not wrong to like humanity." Gwen's own hypocrisy cuts him, but he doesn't care. He understands now, belatedly, what his sister was trying to show him.

"Isn't it, though?" Celdic steps around the desk, closer to Gwen, and Gwen doesn't step back even though that's all he wants to do. The room is large, but it's like the walls are closing in on him. "You know, it wasn't a coincidence that Celeste was gone so often."

The blatant confirmation makes Gwen's eyes widen. "It really was all on purpose?"

"Of course. Did you think Celeste would slip up so easily?"

"So she let Gwendolyn descend. On purpose. And now she's punishing her for descending."

"Yep."

"That still doesn't make any sense," he yells out. "Why did Celeste assign Gwendolyn, or any angel at all, to be a scribe and keep watch over Earth if she knew something like this could happen? What's the point in it all? And why didn't Celeste do anything? Why did she let Gwendolyn continue going down to Earth if—"

Celdic laughs. He laughs and laughs, and it's a terrible, grating sound that makes Gwen's blood boil. "You don't know? You seriously don't know?" He covers his face with his hands, and when he drags them back down, there's an evil glint in his eyes. "Oh, this is just too good."

Gwen scowls, and his nails draw blood from where they dig deeper into his palms. "Just tell me already."

"You're nothing but a shell," Celdic finally says, and everything Gwen feels, all of his anger and frustration, all of it disappears. "You're Celeste's pet project, Gwen. You all are. Gwendolyn, her little mortal friend, all the other angels, even all of Paradisum and Earth—you're just her creations."

He steps forward, towards Gwen, and lifts his chin up with his finger. "Use your brain. She's the God of Space. This world, all these planets, they're just a game to her, a thing to pass time. Common sense, rationality, all that garbage: she doesn't care, Gwen. She never did."

Gwen can't bring himself to move. Finally, he gulps. "You mean … she was just toying with us, with her? The whole time?"

"Bingo. See, I knew you were a bright boy." Celdic turns away and walks over to the window. He beckons Gwen to come watch the view too, and Gwen listens, moving on autopilot.

It's worse than before, if that was even possible; in his peripheral, the cloud floor has deep, jagged cracks that tear through Paradisum, and beneath

63

it all, Earth is more deathly grays and browns than ocean blues and verdant greens. He immediately hones in on the western coast of Europe, where he last saw Gwendolyn, and finds it clouded over by thick smog. "What ... what have you done?"

Celdic smiles again, all sharp teeth. "Oh, I haven't done much. Trust me, if I was down there, you would know. Celeste likes to play with her food more than I do." He paces down the length of the window. "You know," he starts, "I wanted to kill you in front of your sister. But Celeste has her own plans for her and that human."

Gwen doesn't even have a response to that. Nothing feels real, and he's half-convinced that any moment now, he will wake up from this nightmare.

Then, Celdic opens his mouth again: "While it'd be fun to have you watch everything burn, we need to wrap this up soon." He snaps his fingers and something seizes Gwen by the neck. He claws at his throat only to find nothing there. Nothing tangible, at least.

Absently, he recalls a saying the humans have: *when you die, your life flashes before your eyes*. He thinks he's falling to the floor, but he doesn't know because all he can think of is the choking feeling around his neck, and he knows Paradisian angels can't die this easily, surely, they can't, but here he is doing just that, dying like a mortal. Black dots flit across his vision, dancing across the nauseating white of the ceiling. He catches glimpses of something else, too—he sees Paradisum as it used to be: golden and shimmering and ethereal beyond words. He sees his fellow angels living life normally. He sees his sister.

Then it all fades away, and the last thing he sees is Celdic looming over him. "Goodnight, little angel."

THE LAKE OF YOU

by Ruby Chau

As the sun sets over the sea,

I set off on a journey.

The million steps I take

Carry me to the lake.

This is where I cry,

I laugh,

I hide.

This is where I can find my other half.

This is where I write

The millions of poems that bring me to life.

This is where I dream of a miracle

Where all things can be made possible.

My home is not a house.

It is you, without a doubt.

I only feel safe when you are near,

They will never find us here.

EIGHT AM RUMINATIONS OF A SINNER

by *Elem Vu*

It is the first time in years someone has touched you
without trying to kill you.

You call him [   ]
You think he is pretty, so you tell him that,
but pretty is not all there is.
How do you describe all that he gives you?
How do you say thank you for holding me;
thank you for reminding me I am more than my skin;
thank you for showing me I am still here;
thank you for showing me I am not a monster yet?

You do not have the words,

because words have always piled inside you
like something broken and horrible:
a car crash
a muffled sob
a body before it is pushed into its grave.

You do not have the words,

and you will never say the right thing,

especially not to him.

So you call his name and tell him he is pretty,

and you hope it will be enough

even when you know

it never is.

DESIDERIUM

by Jessica Truong

THE FUNERAL IS CLOSED-CASKET.

The case is made of varnished oak wood and adorned with white lilies. It's all oddly artistic, in a way. Akiyo's mother is crouched down, one hand atop the casket and a handkerchief crumpled in the other. Her head is hung low, shoulders shaking as she sobs into her fist.

Akiyo places an assuring palm on his mom's shoulder and gestures for them to go. They leave together, and in the aisle of black outfits and somber expressions, people part for them.

Akiyo's mother has always been a rational person, keeping the family grounded through tough times with gentle yet firm words of affirmation. But death is a concept that scares everyone. Sometimes, in desperation to avoid it, people do horrible things. Other times, it leaves them with an insatiable grief that swallows them whole. His mother falls into the latter.

She refuses to sleep in the same bed as the one her late husband used to, so they've swapped rooms. She says it's a bad omen. Even then, Akiyo always carries her from the living room to the bedroom when she passes out from exhaustion.

Taking care of his despondent mother isn't a chore, but it is draining. It's a child's duty to return the favor to their parents, but nobody can be blamed when alone time is needed—absence makes the heart grow fonder, after all.

Wrapped in a thick scarf and trench coat, Akiyo trudges out to the wooded area near his house. The trees drape over the sky, and gloom hangs in the air. Dew droplets slide off the blades of grass at his shoes.

He's never explored the woods, only skirting the edges of it. He's lived here since he was a child, but what sensible child goes frolicking off in the dark, damp woods with their classmates spreading urban legends around like wildfire? Not Akiyo.

At the end of a winding dirt path, indented by footsteps of those before him, is a beaten-down shrine, bleached from the sun and in a sorry state of disarray. A *torii* gate stands at attention, the faded red still bright against sage. Wandering between the faded *torii* gate, Akiyo closes his eyes in an attempt to keep his breathing at bay.

Then, he's falling—or at least, he feels like it. It's the same heart-stopping feeling of hurtling towards the ground in a dream only to touch solid ground. His head spins, and he catches himself by leaning a hand against the pillars of the gate.

After a moment, he blinks and his eyes refocus. What really throws him off is how dark it has become. He had arrived here early in the morning, so early that the sun had barely begun to peer over the clouds, but everything is now cast in cool, slanted shadows drawn from the spindly boughs of the forest.

He looks back at the dilapidated structure, and his heart leaps in his chest. The sun-bleached wood of the shrine has been replaced by planks tinted a mahogany hue. A thick braid of *shimenawa* rope hangs from the opening to the shrine, adorned with *shinto* symbols. A *torii* gate stands nearby, painted a bright shade of red with the same *shimenawa* rope strung across its pillars.

A figure slides the shrine door open, her thin face drawn in a startled expression. She wears a white *kosode* and a scarlet *hakama*, the sleeves stitched with crimson threads. She's ghostly pale, vermillion lips and winged red liner underneath her eyes standing out like blood on snow. Inky black hair

69

cascades down her shoulders and falls down in thick tresses. She resembles a shrine maiden, the ones he'd see when they'd go to ring the bell for New Years. Cautiously, she treads to him, gliding across the grass.

Akiyo hesitates, words caught in his throat. "Hello. Sorry, was that always there?" He nods towards the new structures.

"You're human?" she asks, disregarding his lackluster introduction.

What does that mean? Akiyo clears his throat. "O-of course. What else would I be?"

Her eyes go wide and her crimson lips part. "That's odd. You're new here."

"New?"

She nods as if he just reaffirmed her suspicions. Her angular features somehow translate over to a softer expression when she smiles, eyes crinkling into gentle crescents.

"My name is Makoto." She extends a slender hand. Her fingernails are filed down to a sharp point.

Akiyo shakes it politely. "Akiyo. Nice to meet you. Sorry, do you mind explaining what you said earlier? Human?"

Makoto purses her lips. "Perhaps … it is best you see it yourself."

* * *

The forest is dark, painted by deep shades of juniper and sage. As one subjected to pareidolia would start to imagine faces in everyday objects, Akiyo can feel the hairs on the back of his neck stand on their ends.

The forest feels alive, breathing and bristling in the beat of his and Makoto's footsteps. Flickers of blue flames dance in his peripheral vision; his mother's tales of *hitodama* ring in his ears. If he remembered correctly, *hitodama* were souls detached from the human body.

If his eyes strayed from Makoto's figure for too long, he'd begin to see

70

anguished faces in the trunks of the trees. Makoto's pure white *kosode* is stark against the backdrop of the night. Akiyo keeps a little closer to her. She feels the warmth of his body growing closer and clasps a hand over her mouth to stifle a chuckle, amused at his wariness.

They talk in hushed voices—Akiyo doesn't understand why, but the ominous atmosphere of the woods pushes him to follow her lead. Because of the high *getas* she wears on her feet, her ankles roll against an ill-timed pebble. Akiyo catches her by the arm when she trips, helping her up again. She rests a dainty hand on his forearm as she regains her footing.

She flutters her eyelashes at him in an exaggerated manner. "Why trust me so easily, Akiyo?" Makoto asks. "Surely, it's not shallow attraction."

"Innocent until proven guilty, right?" Akiyo responds. "That's what my mom taught me to live by. Besides, you haven't done anything wrong."

"You aren't afraid I could be a murderer?" A benign smile curls her lips up, playful.

"Are you?"

Makoto laughs it off. "No, but it's very kind of you to hand me your trust. You're very thoughtful."

She gently grabs his hand and pulls him off the path, to venture deeper into the forest. Her footsteps are silent, her *hakama* flowing as she gracefully steps through the brush. Akiyo, who is unfamiliar with the environment and clumsier relative to her, somehow manages to step on every dry leaf and twig on the ground.

Makoto grabs his coat, yanking him to the ground and dragging him into a bush. She leans against a tree, crouched into a hiding position. Akiyo opens his mouth to speak, but she holds her index finger up to her lips. *Quiet.* The only thing he can hear is the wind: the whispering of the leaves as they move against each other, the almost inaudible sound of wings rustling.

Akiyo stiffens and crouches down even lower. His gaze is cast to the ground, but Makoto lifts his chin up so that he can peek through the

71

openings in the bush. Makoto looks almost too comfortable with the woods, pleasant smile posed on her face and posture relaxed. There is a figure in the distance, too dark for him to determine the gender, but he can see large wings protruding from its back. It searches, slowly moving around every tree like a predator on the prowl. Akiyo is worried it might hear his own pounding heartbeat.

Then, with wings extended, it shoots up into the sky with one powerful motion. There in the moonlight, Akiyo could make out the features of an old man with a large, crooked nose. Makoto pulls him back up again. "Do you know what that was?"

Akiyo shakes his head, afraid to speak.

Makoto stands up and continues, "It was a *tengu*. They lure Buddhists off the path of enlightenment through promises of teaching their tricks. A bit of a devious *youkai*, don't you agree?"

"*Youkai*?" Akiyo parrots quietly. "Aren't they just urban folklore? Like children's tales?"

Makoto laughs, a sound that chimes like church bells. "I didn't believe it either. Not many truly believe they actually exist. In here though, there are many. They're quite mischievous. Do your best to avoid them."

"Is … is this not the real world?" Akiyo asks. "Where are we?"

"You can guess by now, right? I haven't been gone long enough to find out that the fall of human intelligence is imminent."

Akiyo is silent. Makoto smiles. "You're a little slow right now. It's the spirit world. All late people lingering in limbo come to roam this world until they're able to return to finish business. But more often than not, *youkai* will rip that opportunity away from them to inflict chaos upon the waking world. It's amusing."

At Akiyo's stunned expression, Makoto laughs. "Don't look so surprised. Surely, you didn't expect a *tengu*, of all things, to be roaming around willy-nilly without the army trying to hunt it down."

72

"I don't …"

Makoto leads him out of the thick brush of the forest. "It's nothing to be embarrassed about. I'm sure any human would be shocked."

* * *

They get time to learn more about one another, though Makoto is hesitant to share the life she had before she became trapped in this realm.

"No need to say anything," Akiyo reassures her. "I understand that some people are more private than others."

Taken aback, she is quiet for a long time. Something akin to guilt swirls in her eyes, but when she blinks, it's gone.

She is kind, overwhelmingly so. In the days Akiyo has spent idling the *torii* gate that cursed him to the spirit world, she's stuck by him so closely that it's starting to feel suffocating. It's not that he doesn't enjoy her company— she's bewitchingly beautiful and a well of knowledge—but he can feel her eyes cut through him even when his head is turned.

"Are you lonely, Makoto?" Akiyo says one day.

She tilts her head, startled. "Sorry?"

He looks away. "You've just … been really attentive to me. Is there something wrong? Like anything you want to say?"

She blushes, carding through her hair. "No. It's nothing. I just … really like your company. Is that wrong?"

Akiyo's face burns. He's not even sure if he likes her in a romantic way, but something about her lures him in, like fish to bait. In another life, he wouldn't have doubted that she had been a siren or some other mythical being made to entrance foolish men.

"Nothing wrong," he exclaims. "I think I'm just used to being alone, you know?"

Makoto nods. "I understand."

When Akiyo turns away again, she raises her head to the dark sky, endlessly black. Her premature apology is left unspoken.

* * *

On the seventh day, Akiyo finally kicks at the dirt, staring hard at the moss on the trees. "Makoto, I know you don't like talking about it, but is there any way out of here?"

She sighs, but for once in the week that he's spent with her, she answers the question. "There is. I just think it's impossible to do."

Akiyo jumps at the response. "I have to try. My mom's still out there alone. I can't leave her. Not after …" Makoto's curious gaze bores into him, urging him to continue. "Not after she just lost my dad."

"I'm sorry." Her voice is earnest. In the resounding beat of silence, Makoto takes a breath and adds, "The universe operates on an 'an eye for an eye' type of system. If you kill a *youkai* in this world, you are then able to exchange their life for a return to the human world, which is essentially your own life. I was hesitant to tell you. It's a fool's errand, but you seem like the type to ignore that. Just know this: it's impossible. Humans have no business being able to kill *youkai*—at least, not without any tricks up their sleeves."

"How long have you been stuck here?" Akiyo asks.

She averts her gaze. "Keeping track of time is hard here, but it's been a while since I last saw a human."

He takes her hands and laces them with his own. He gives her a smile. "We can work together then, so we can both return home. Two heads are better than one."

Her gaze is burning. "And if one of us has to be left behind?"

Akiyo gnaws on his lip. He knows what has to happen, but it hurts to say. "I'll stay behind if need be. You've been gone for too long. I'm sure there'll be a chance for me to escape."

When Akiyo turns back to the direction of the path, out of earshot, Makoto whispers to the wind, "He is a lot kinder than most humans."

* * *

"I can be bait," Akiyo says, voice firm. Makoto looks up, sitting criss-cross near the *torii*. "You can come in from behind and do whatever it is that the youkai is vulnerable to. Surely, they wouldn't give up a chance to walk in the living world again."

She rests her cheek against her palm, unimpressed. "That's ridiculous," she responds. "Why place so much on your own life?"

"Well, we *have* to get you out somehow."

"Maybe this was a bad idea. I think you should be the one to go. You do have a family waiting for you."

He gives her an unamused stare and looks up. "You've been here long enough where you can't even tell me when you first got here. It's cruel to have you wait any longer. Why are *you* so adamant on staying?"

"Maybe I like it here," she tries. It's not very convincing.

He retorts with another question, but he only gets silence in response. When he looks back at her, she's gone.

His immediate thought is that she went back to the shrine—she spends most of her time sitting inside, lost in thought.

He walks into the shrine, closes the door behind him, and squints into the darkness. The candles are not lit, and he calls out hesitantly, "Makoto?"

It is dead silent, and Akiyo feels behind him to look for the door.

A hand grabs his wrist, the grip bruising, and he tries yanking it back when another hand wraps around his throat.

Something digs into his skin, and he struggles to escape its grip. A candle flickers to life, bathing the small shrine in warm light. Makoto stands behind him, ghostly white and face distinctly more fox-like. Two ears poke

75

up from the top of her head, and multiple tails are flared out behind her.

But then her grip loosens, face slack in frustration. "I ... can't kill you."

Akiyo stumbles back, falling onto the floor in fear. Sounding braver than he feels, he asks, "You can't? Or you won't?"

"I won't." Makoto sits down, the claws on her hands thinly veiled in his blood. Her face crumples in anger and frustration, her eyes squeezing shut. A hot tear leaks out despite herself, and she lets it trail down her blanched face.

"It's ridiculous. You are the first to give me your trust so easily. I didn't even have to trick you. Every man who's frolicked in here has died by their own arrogance, and the *youkai* pity me because I keep getting my chance at a new life stolen," Makoto spits out. "Can you believe that? *Kitsunes* are meant to be powerful, and yet I'm folding to the first man that'll show me kindness."

The *kitsune* spirit points to a corner of the shrine, stacked with blankets and wooden boxes. "There is a knife underneath the floor. Sacrifice me here. I've been trapped here for too long to wait for more scum to walk through the gates."

At her command, Akiyo shakily pushes aside the sheets and boxes to open the floorboards. There is, in fact, a knife with an intricately carved handle. The blade gleams in the dark. Akiyo's mouth is still open, speechless and dagger trembling in his fist. "I don't ... I don't want to kill you. You've been nothing but kind to me. It's not fair."

Makoto laughs sadly. It's horrifying to know how much the *kitsune* had fooled him with her tender nature and graceful looks, but now, the sound is bitter, grating against his ears. Fooled and toyed with, he should be home already, having stabbed her, but here he is, unable to enact the revenge Makoto is granting him.

She casts her gaze to the floor. "Life isn't fair. You must take the opportunities you're given, Akiyo. Go home to your mother. No doubt she is awaiting you. Time works differently here. It has not been as long as you think."

Akiyo holds it to her neck, pressing. A thin trail of blood rolls down, and it seeps through the *kosode*. Her face is relaxed and melancholic— resigned to both her fate and the young man who's been too selfless for a stranger. Her hands rest atop his, and she guides him to press it deeper. The blade pierces her neck, cascades of blood running down, and it's as morbidly beautiful as she is.

He rests his forehead against hers, and by the time he's evened out his breathing, the dagger is out of his hands, and he is kneeling in the ramshackle shrine, old and forgotten. The sun shines through the open door.

It is morning. Another day has come, and Makoto is now another memory he must carry.

GODHOOD IN AMERICA

by Elem Vu

say you are a god.

say you awaken one day and find yourself on earth.
you are helpless and fragile and even mortal.

you love your parents

but they break so easily.

they know so little about you

yet so much about being human.

they cannot believe sanctitude does not follow the constraints of man.

they say you are mortal.

they say you are definable by human terms.

they and everyone else wish to constrain your godhood:

to crumple your wings into human form,

rewrite your name for their mouths,

warp your body to fit into what is right,

what is human.

say you play along with their games.

say you choke down your sanctity and bury it deep

and force yourself to forget.

so here you are,

            perfectly human and earthly,

until swallowing divinity makes you sick.

here you are:

            throwing up in the kitchen sink,

            hoping your humanity will come up instead,

pseudo-Prometheus ripping yourself apart

            only for some curse to heal you anew.

say man is your ruler now.

man takes away your godhood.

so what are you now, godling?

            broken,

                  ruined,

                          wrong.

what can you do, fallen deity?

man picks apart the corpse of your holiness.

man decides to hunt you for sport.

                        man devises laws meant to kill you,

                      he makes laws in the name of justice,

                          in the name of what is right.

because you, dear divinity,

are an abomination

            a violation of nature

                        unnatural

          confused

              delusional

etcetera

etcetera.

whatever you are,

you are not human;

you are a monster,

and monsters do not deserve to live.

mankind is greedy,

mankind is cruel,

to take even when we have nothing to give;

we were once everything,

and now?

tell us, humanity,

what are you so afraid of?

divinity or deviation?

sanctity or sacrilege?

piety or the profound?

tell us, fearful ones,

was there ever a difference between those to you?

have you spent so long in darkness that you lost your sight?

did the stolen fire come too late?

tell us, humankind,

what, if anything, have we done wrong?

what atrocity have we committed,

other than existing,

to earn your ire?

does your fear have a reason? a name?

tell us, ignorant ones,

was it ever fear at all?

THE MONSTERS YOU HAVE MADE OF GODS WANT TO KNOW,

WERE WE NOT HOLY ONCE?

A MOTHER'S LOVE

by Kellan Nguyen

When he was born, you wanted a kind child.
A soft child, one who wouldn't laugh so abrasively
Or talk too loudly.
A strong child, one who would not give up so easily
Nor fall apart too quickly.
You wanted a sweet child, a healthy child, a happy child
But you did not want your son.

Yet he is all you have, and in him
You see traces of your own face—
The way his eyes crinkle when he laughs,
The dimples at the creases of his toothy smile,
And everything, everything, *everything*
You hate about yourself.

You try to love him anyway.
Just like how he is all you have, you are all he has,
And you can't abandon him,
A mistake repeated far too many times.

You tell him you love him,

That he's all you've ever wanted in a child,

And he smiles at you, arms stretched wide for a hug,

Yet you cannot help but hate him all the same.

You wanted him to be sweet and healthy and happy

Because you wanted him to be better than you,

Someone who was everything you are not.

But he is your son and you are his mother,

So he will always be everything you hate,

And when you tell him, *I love you,* over and over,

You will never mean it.

GLIMPSE OF A KALEIDOSCOPE

by Jeslyn Le

IN THE KALEIDOSCOPE of my memories I remember times that have long since passed, little crushes of color and prismatic shards that bear the scarcest glimpses into the worlds we used to roam. I remember autumn leaves crunching brittle beneath our feet as I chased you across the asphalt, leaves that fell incessantly from the air, the streaks of blood-red and dry umber that followed in our wake, a painting of sorts, warm, falling, then swept away in a tumultuous gust of air that rushed deep into my lungs and invisibly cut a path around me to fly out to the rest of the world.

You were always two or three steps ahead, and no matter how hard I pushed myself, no matter how intensely my muscles burned, I could never catch up to you. I didn't mind, though. It was your vibrant laughter ringing through the air I was chasing after.

On one month in particular you were opening an umbrella we'd borrowed from the elderly woman in the neighborhood while mine dangled in my hand, unused. Cold rain streamed steadily down our faces. It splashed onto the earth, too, and the cobbled road that led to your home. Rain on the rooftops, rain on the windowpanes, raindrops balanced delicately on thin blades of grass … the whole world was alive.

You hated the rain, solely because it threatened to dampen your socks and your favorite sweater, while I took delight in the way it stung my cheeks and left countless reflective puddles in its wake. Each and every one we came across was inevitably met with the swift kick of my boot. You were quite aggravated at the time, though partway through your complaints you fell eerily silent. When I finally thought to ponder it, you had gone from using the elderly woman's umbrella as a shield against the rain to a gleaming polka-dotted sword, which you swung with the fury of a thousand suns at my unsuspecting ribcage.

Instead of going to your house straight away like we had originally intended, we spent quite some time in pursuit of one another amid the rain. At some points we nearly fell splat on the cobblestones trying to mercilessly pummel one another with our weaponized umbrellas. But that was all part of the fun.

Yes, I recall having a visceral love for nature's blessings. It was the sole love I had for anything before we found each other. When I was alone and cried often, I ran into the arms of the spring fronds, who would receive me without judgement. Those fronds would cover me, would murmur to one another as they peered into the little dirt crib I hollowed out for myself, and while I lay aching for the warmth of another, the sunlight would descend through the leaves like an invisible angel to cradle my drooping head and wrap me in its embrace.

That's why, when we finally found each other—or perhaps it's more accurate to say when you found *me*—I wanted to share these mundane treasures with you.

Aside from the rain (you never could get over how soaked your socks became), you indulged in my eagerness to share this world that had raised me so tenderly. Together, we investigated all that it had to offer, and, in turn, discovered parts of ourselves that had otherwise gone neglected. First, we were cartographers tracing calloused fingers across the portraiture of our most beloved Mother Nature; in the same instant we were explorers braving perilous roads, mountaineers scaling grand canyons in the blazing sun, sailors adrift between uncharted peninsulas, everything, everywhere, all at once.

At first, I only intended to give you a glimpse into my world. With enough time you became a part of it. In the midst of the spring fronds, the autumn leaves and rain, idling on rocky edges and coasting between tropical islands, there you were—the centerpiece of every picture, nature's most brilliant creation, my dearly beloved friend.

To this day, I lie here thinking about you. Are you still out there somewhere, listening? Are you? It doesn't matter if you are. It is, in all technicality, impossible for you to, but I want to say it anyway. I love you so much.

All beings who exist with the power to nurture possess the strength to hurt as well. It was something I had easily forgotten and something you hardly considered. Still, what happened wasn't my fault, and it wasn't yours either. We were both simply too young to understand it at the time.

The earliest imprint of such a message revealed itself on our first trip together to a land blanketed in snow. Unlike all the other territories, which burst at the seams with colors of every kind, this one was muted and trapped in a pale haze of lavender and periwinkle.

You and I, alongside the thin and lonely shadows scattered across the expanse, were the sole inhabitants of this empty canvas. But when had something like that ever bothered us? When we joined hands, we painted a universe entirely of our own making.

Having never seen such a landscape before, we spent much of the time absorbing our surroundings in a dazed stupor, while only a portion of the rest was spent exploring and playing in the snow. It hadn't been long before we found something of special interest. Behind us rose the snow-capped silhouette of the cabin whose eyes we hadn't yet escaped, and there in front of us was a small frozen lake shining with a deep cobalt sheen. In a ring around the lake were dozens of scattered snowdrops that had strayed farther from the trees.

We turned to each other, both of us lost in silent wonder, then back to the stretch of ice before us. Your eyes gleamed—you urged me to take a closer look. And what else was there to do but oblige?

As we neared its frigid surface, I paused and inhaled slowly. You offered to go first, but I shook my head decisively. I exhaled. A soft cloud dissolved into the mist. Then, I carefully toed the edge of the lake. It seemed thick enough. After a light hesitance, my right boot made full contact with the ice.

Next, the left boot. Right. Left. Right. Left. Right. Left. Right …

I heard your voice cheering me on not too far away. My legs wobbled, and I heard a stiff creak. How far had I gone? Not that far at all. Ah, hold on a minute. Here, it seemed a bit—

"Boo!"

In my shock, I stumbled forward. The ice split open from the extra weight that struck down on it; instantly, my senses were overwhelmed by the sheer cold, the weight of my limbs, the void of dark water stretching endlessly beneath me. Oh. This was it. I was going to die. I was definitely going to die. I felt it for certain …

I awoke to a dim and quiet room. Lamplight flickered in the corner of my vision. There was no other presence save for your aunt, who had just arrived with a warm bowl of porridge. When she saw me struggling to sit up, she set the bowl on the nightstand nearby, propped me against the pillows, and placed a cool hand on my forehead to check for my temperature. Then after a minute or so she left to call you, who swiftly appeared at the door frame and whose outline cast a long shadow against the yellow rectangle of light emitted from the room beyond.

When you drew closer, you moved to hug me, paused midway, thought better of it, and resolved to stand at a comfortable distance by my bedside. I watched you attentively while you averted your eyes.

Neither of us spoke at first.

Inevitably, it was you who broke the silence. Even as the words tumbled out of your mouth, you never once looked at me. You told me you were sorry, so sorry. It was all your fault, it was stupid of you, you hadn't meant to, I could've died and if your aunt and uncle hadn't been so close by—

Stop! Stop, that was enough. Above all I was taken aback at the tremor that disturbed your voice, because out of all the particularly striking emotions you'd shown throughout the years, not once had I ever seen you express such a clear and palpable sorrow. As if that wasn't enough, you continued to apologize over and over, perhaps taking my interruption as a rejection, and as badly as I wanted to grab your hand, to smile and tell you that it was all okay, the only other image that surfaced at your unsteady mantra was the bitter shock that stabbed every inch of my body when I fell into the water.

If it had been any other time in any other place, I could have easily reassured you in spite of the unfamiliarity of the situation. Here, however, within the cabin lost in a snowscape next to the gloomy lamplight and its flickering shadows, I found that there was nothing I could do in the face of your sadness. After enough time, you went from pleading for forgiveness to covering your face with your hands.

You cried. I couldn't understand why. I was alive, wasn't I? I was right here. And besides, I was the one who fell, so shouldn't I have been crying instead?

"Come here," I wanted to say. "Give me a hug. It's okay. It'll be okay."

But I couldn't say anything. Currents of water swirled steadily in my ears.

Soon afterwards, I came down with an awful fever. In the remaining days I spent bedridden, none of my family came to visit. The only visitors I had were your aunt and uncle, who checked on me frequently and stayed throughout the night to ensure that no issues arose. They were shockingly kind people. It's a shame, I thought as I watched them shuffle quietly in the night, that neither of us could see them that often. And it was an even bigger shame, I continued to myself, that you were nowhere to be found in this room with them. A surge of heat rushed to my head.

You weren't going to visit. But why? Where were you? What were you doing? Why wouldn't you come? Was it because I failed to accept your apology? I sulked incessantly. It wouldn't have felt so terrible if you hadn't left me here to recover on my own. If I was in the right state of mind, I would've forgiven you instantly. Didn't you know that? If only you came to see me again, then maybe I'd have another chance to tell you I wasn't angry with you.

I stared at the ceiling. While doing so I turned these thoughts over in my head, inspected them from every angle with the same intensity and dismal bleariness I did counting all the cobwebs that strung across the corners of the cabin as wispy floating strands. You were sad. You were afraid. You cried in front of me for the first time, and now you were avoiding me.

Thinking back on it, you were always a bright and oddly adaptable person. The only complaints you ever had were for the minute matters, and whenever it came to my attention that you were even the slightest bit perturbed, you were quick to brush it aside with a revitalized joviality. It struck me as odd at first, but the more I thought about it, the more I seemed to understand. Your resilience was carefully crafted. There were still parts of yourself you hadn't yet given away, parts I was never aware existed in the first place.

In your white-knuckled grasp, you held a mirror that reflected the entire world, and the visions within the glass were so lovely, so fascinating, so frighteningly beautiful that I forgot to ask whether those hands of yours ached holding it up for so long, forgot to wonder altogether about the face obscured behind it.

It occurred to me that even you had things you were afraid to lose.

* * *

Years later, on a day when the entire world seemed to roll on endlessly in lush, verdant green, I recall rushing to meet you at the border of the forest we used to play in together. I was running late, and I didn't want you to think

I had gone and forgotten all about you, so like a frenzied spurt of flame I sped across the tall, swaying fields and spent many a moment nearly tripping over my own feet in the futile hope that I would somehow still make it there at an acceptable time.

When I arrived, I saw nothing but a bench and the thicket of weary trees that crowded behind it. They spanned across my entire line of sight, just a few feet shy of the worn wood and its flaking paint as if they, too, had been informed in advance of my urgent arrival and had all been convinced to step back to make room for my increasingly anxious presence.

Young buds peered at me curiously from the safety of the branches. There were also clusters of tulips, baby's-breaths, daffodils and daisies, all of which trembled delicately under the lightest of breezes and waved to me as I stood feeling somewhat out of place against the backdrop of the sunlit clearing. Everything else was here, but where were you? You were nowhere to be seen. A hint of bile threatened to rise from the back of my throat. No, no, absolutely not. What was I thinking?

I decided to wait for you on the bench. Upon my approach, I found taped firmly to its backrest a crisp white note splashed in shimmering sunlight. The contents of the note read:

Come find me!

Then, scribbled hastily beneath that message:

Look under the bench!

I followed its directions promptly. In the space beneath the bench lay a smooth, grey pebble, and marked on its surface in black paint was an arrow pointing northward … I could see where this was going.

You left few other traces. Another rock every now and then, and, if the mood struck you, an etching in the tree over there. The rest was up to interpretation.

On the path to you, I was met with a collection of precious sights. Hints of sky above the canopy, remarkably blue, wreaths of ivory blossoms that wound around numerous overlapping branches. Cool shadows dotted by rippling golden rays, thrushes in the trees, gently curled ferns, and to my wonder and delight, I discovered that the entirety of the forest I had traversed as a child bloomed anew in an utterly breathtaking and unfamiliar transformation of the landscape.

Life, everywhere. The culmination of sunshine and every fond feeling in the world. The daisies followed me deeper down the woods, yellow faces bright with the vitality only a newborn could have, and alongside them were the wood poppies, who craned forward in a mischievous attempt to nip at the soles of my shoes. I knelt down and greeted them with a smile—how I adored them! I'd sit with them forever, given the chance. On the other hand, you ...

You had grown tired of the spring. That was what you'd told me the previous season as we lay sprawled beneath an overcast sky.

It was tempting, the thought of staying here for just a while longer, but there was someone waiting for me.

After many turns, the trail came to a hard stop at the foot of a small oak tree, one that bordered the opening to a vibrant field. The final sign that appeared before me was a neatly carved heart. As I stared at it in deep puzzlement, a suspicious rustling sounded from the branches behind me. Next came a resounding thud, and before I had time to question what was happening there as well, you plucked a stray leaf off the top of my head and spun me around to face you.

"Surprise!" you shouted gleefully. "Since you took so long I decided I'd come up with a little something to relieve my boredom. I couldn't help myself, so ..."

Your voice trailed off sheepishly. I flicked your forehead in a mixture of exasperation and amusement. You really never could.

"So, how was it?" you asked me. "Did you have fun?"

Oh, of course I did. Every second drafted in your design was an adventure. At the same time, some part of me wished we could have walked all the way here together. I never spent nearly as much time with you as I wanted to anymore.

* * *

I remember another day when you led me away from the seashore. You held my hands in a vice-like grip. Every step I took forward was your step backward, and the rushes of indigo and deep navy that struck our legs burst into oddly patterned whorls of seafoam, then into wondrous fractals swept off by the incoming tides, converging, blooming, splitting, washed away.

The rocking of the waves made me thoroughly nauseous. As we waded further into the darkening expanse, I loathed myself, the foolhardy self who believed for even a second that this was a good idea, and more importantly loathed the you of that moment, who had so eagerly insisted to me that it was safe. There was a point unnoticed in the midst of my petulance and self-reproach when our feet finally left the sand to float in the water.

At that exact moment, a newly formed wave crested over us.

It was small, and objectively unimpressive; despite this rationale, my heart shuddered violently in its wake. When both of our visions were swallowed by the glimmering blue wall, you shouted something at me, and I shouted something back, though thinking about it now I can't remember what it was, and even then I couldn't make sense of it, for every sound that came out of your mouth was drowned by a distant thunder deep within my chest.

Then, as silently and calmly as it had risen, the ominous wave crashed down on us. My eyes squeezed shut. In the next moment you were holding me. Holding me tightly, holding me with a startling desperation ...

Together we plummeted beneath the ocean's gently rocking waters, twin embryos tangled in a glacial womb, the cord of your arms squeezing my neck as comforting as it was suffocating. I couldn't move. I couldn't breathe. I thought to myself that this was fine, that this was alright, because against all feeling, I still believed you would carry me to safety.

At the same time, I wanted to cry out and struggle, not against the waves but against you, who had brought me here against my will, wanted to tear myself away from your embrace, to scream "I told you this wasn't going to work!" and return to the surface where the heathered clouds waited all by my lonesome. In simpler terms, I was absolutely livid.

Still, I trusted you. It would have been a betrayal of my very being not to trust you.

In the blink of an eye, we were back under the open sky.

* * *

Come to think of it, when was the last time we spoke to one another? Was it the argument we had at the foot of a staircase? Or was it the time we passed each other at a train station, uttered a brief "hello" and continued walking our separate ways?

When I think of "finality," I think of the final pages of a storybook, of death and its infinite darkness after the split-second flash of a flame we call life. There was no ending between the two of us. For a time, we revolved around each other, two globes on a wobbling axis, then in the same way the Moon pulls away from the Earth every year we slowly drifted off into distant space, lost to the cosmos, leaving behind all but a gaping black space the two of us used to fill.

Our memories are the only record of that time now. The cogs of my mind rotate slowly, the kaleidoscope turns with it, large projections searing millions of colors into a tall, blank wall that I lie down and watch every now and then. When I feel particularly lonely, you join me as well, a specter living purely within the psychedelic headlights. We laugh together, cry together, talk for hours like we always have. When we're done, we shake hands and bow to one another. You return to the wall behind the projection, and I return to my current life without you.

It's not an unhappy life by any means. It remains tinged with the scent of dewdrops, filled with the endless vitality of spring, warm with sunshine, red with autumn leaves, cold with the first frost of winter and every other piece of the world we reveled in.

Sometimes I sit by the window and watch the people who roam the streets below. I see whorls of lavender petals hanging from the garland above my window, the rolling morning mist as it's set ablaze by sunlight falling in hazy golden rays along the pavement. There's the boy racing down the street with his dog. Between two buildings lies the pitch black of an alleyway a young man slips into. Sparrows dot the rooftops, a woman by the fountain plays her violin. Steam curls from the cup of coffee that rests neglected on the table, the world is peaceful and while I'm here, sitting by the window, I know I am at ease.

I miss you. That's all.

WHAT I POUR MY HEART INTO

by Jenny Nguyen

I draw with blood.
Nails chipped,
Eyes crazed.

My desires
Course through my veins,
Burning me.

My fingers snap off,
My eyes roll out,
My blood runs still.

Slow down.
Oh, heartbeat,
Slow down.

My last breath
Shall breathe *it* to life.
And what a masterpiece
It will be.

My lovely, my beautiful
My final creation.

PARTING

by Jeslyn Le

A wave
Resounds against the muddy shore
Swirling in rivulets around my ankles

my arms
my neck
my shoulders, spilling into crevices
largely neglected,

Filling empty chasms which echo every envy,
Caressing every darkened bruise
And laying cool kisses along my aching spine
And worn hands

It crashes against me
Overwhelmingly, suddenly,
Prying open the cavern of my mouth

to quench
to fill
to collapse against

a parched throat

a hole in my soul

a still-beating heart

Its embrace is cold, but its sentiments are warm.

Eventually, it slips through my fingers.

Every frigid tear returns to the expanse.

So this is how you feel?

SEE YOU NEXT TIME!

by Jeslyn Le

Bleeding molten gold,
The city nightscape whispers
Its final farewell.

STARCROSSED

by Kevin Nguyen

A star dances above the lake,
My weary eyes twitch in slumber
To the forms which I create
In such dreams I've fallen under.

I wake up in twilight fog,
Misty tunes across the stars.
Endless haze of midnight smog,
No one knows just where we are.

In the shadows, I see your face,
Asleep in dreams at dawn unbroken.
In this sky we can't embrace
Are words best left unspoken.

Now this star is all but gone,
I'll remember from here on.

AUTHOR BIOS

Ruby Chau

Originally from Saigon, Ruby Chau moved to the United States when she was twelve. In high school, she discovered a passion for reading books and dancing. She also developed an interest in biology. After graduating, Ruby wants to major in medicine and hopes to become a physician assistant.

Orbal Farhad

A first-time published author, Orbal Farhad is a junior at La Quinta High School. Farhad grew up with a natural gravitation towards writing and performing. She is excited for her future, and plans on eventually extending her short stories, including Petra, into longer works.

Ethan Ho

Born in California, Ethan Ho lives in Garden Grove where he discovered many cultures and outdoor activities, and unearthed a passion for science. Writing since primary school, his first published story is "Torrential Events." Ethan hopes to be a scientist in the field of aeronautics.

Jeslyn Le

Jeslyn Le was born in Fountain Valley and raised in Westminster. Although she focuses on her artwork above all other creative endeavors, she has nurtured a steady love for writing and developed many stories in her spare time. Her first published story is "Glimpse of a Kaleidoscope."

Kevin Le

Kevin Le was raised in Westminster, California where he developed a love for performing arts, practicing music, and making people laugh. He is known to appear when "I stayed up too late and now it's 3:00 AM" is whispered into the dark three times.

Teresa Le

Teresa Le has a PhD in procrastination. She was born in Fountain Valley, California and currently resides in Santa Ana. She adores the colors blue and brown, and has a Squishmallow addiction. She serves as President of the Creative Writing Club and her smile can brighten any day.

Jenny Nguyen

Jenny Nguyen absolutely loves anime, manhwa, and video games. She's terrified of blood but reads and watches bloody battles anyway. She's in her first year of high school. "What I Pour My Heart Into" and "What We've Done" are her first published works.

Kellan Nguyen

Kellan Nguyen is an artist, author, and future scientist. This is their third year in Creative Writing, and they've written short stories, poems, and outlined future novels about their characters. Even though they'll be studying physics at university, they'll always cherish the arts and writing.

Kevin Nguyen

Born in Washington and raised in California, Kevin Nguyen is an aspiring writer. His only goal in life is to have a pet. At least, that's the plan for now. He likes listening to music of all genres, drawing whatever comes to mind, and bothering his friends.

Audrey Pham

Audrey Pham grew up in Garden Grove where she fell in love with cross country, reading short stories, and finally writing her own. She's enjoyed writing for a decade, but "In Plain Sight" and "Dear Ammie" are her first published stories. Audrey hopes to become an orthodontist.

Jessica Truong

Jessica Truong, born in Vietnam and raised in SoCal, loves basketball, writing, and art, both traditional and digital. She aspires to become a pediatrician and not allow her favorite NBA team's final score decide her day. "Desiderium" and "For I Have Sinned" are her first published works.

Iman Usman

Originally from California, Iman Usman grew up in Garden Grove where she developed her love for writing and drawing. Her passion for art shows up in many of her writing, her favorite topic being nature. She aspires to pursue her dream of becoming a Software Engineer.

Tracy Vo

Local cryptid Tracy Vo can be found skulking around the Westminster area, frequently sighted in school parking lots and retail stores. Witnesses report having seen her engage in activities such as digital painting, but no recent evidence has been discovered to reveal what exactly she is plotting.

Elem Vu

Elem Vu is a high school senior. He spends his time reading poetry and drawing his original characters. Elem also enjoys baking. He has an interest in literature and biology.

Vivian Vu

Born in Fountain Valley and raised in Westminster, Vivian Vu loves literature and writing. Initially, she focused on writing short stories but now works on novels and novellas. Her favorite character, Alastor, debuts in her first published story, "Enemy Grounds."

Hailey Zuniga

Born in California, Hailey Zuniga grew up in Westminster where she found a love for writing, dance, and art. She has been writing since the fourth grade, with her most recent works published being "Forgetfulness" and "Where I'm From." In the future, Hailey hopes to become a teacher.

www.ingramcontent.com/pod-product-compliance
Lightning Source LLC
Chambersburg PA
CBHW050803250626
47155CB00005B/2198